MAIN EVENT

MAIN EVENT

J.L. MINYARD

CENTURION
BOOKS

MAIN EVENT © 2025 by Jessica Minyard

hello@jessicaminyard.com

Cover by Cormar Covers

Interior graphics by mgsdesiigns / eBook map design by Books and Moods

Editing by Erica Edits

http://www.ericaedits.com/

ISBN: 978-1-957004-15-0

eBook ISBN: 978-1-957004-14-3

20250621

CONTENT NOTES

This book contains material that may be sensitive to some readers.

CWs: explicit sex and language, blood and minor injuries, light elements of kink and BDSM, pregnancy and associated symptoms, postpartum anxiety, brief religious discussions, brief mention of abortion, unprotected sex, pregnancy and breeding kinks.

For the mothers.

Introduction

Rituals

When it's time for bed, we take refuge in the big blue recliner, stretched out, belly to belly, little feet touching my knees. I was so afraid the mass of my body would prevent me from holding you close enough. You don't seem to mind the gentle roll.

Your little finger points, asking, *What's this, what's this.*

Lamp, curtains, fan, chin, mouth, nose, forehead. Forehead is extremely funny, as is me nibbling that questing finger that wants to know so much.

Your laugh, high-pitched and silver, clear as glass, heavy and somber like a church bell, washes me clean, salvation.

I wrap you up, feel the wings of your shoulder blades, feel the soft exhalations of your breathing, feel my own breathing slow to match yours, tuning.

I squeeze tighter to hold you here, in this space between baby and child, a blue-eyed blonde sun, radiant.

Staring burns me up from the inside out, ashes to ashes, reborn.

Jessica Minyard, 2021

Chapter One
Shyanne

Another Friday night and another fruitless date from the internet.

Shyanne had meant to deactivate her profile months ago, but she'd forgotten and then she'd matched with Josh, the man across the table from her, currently eating the last breadstick and finishing his pitcher of Miller Lite.

The wafting smell of the beer was making Shyanne nauseous, but she managed to keep her face mostly pleasant. At least, she hoped it was pleasant. Josh wasn't paying that much attention to her face. His eyes kept straying to the cleavage exposed by the square neckline of her dark green velvet cocktail dress.

Shyanne liked this dress. She felt comfortable and confident in this dress, even if it was getting a little tight around the middle. No one could really tell, not yet.

The green dress was her designated first date outfit, and it usually went over very well. Josh was a fan, even though Shyanne would appreciate it if he'd eventually look elsewhere. Like her face.

She shouldn't have agreed to the date. She knew better, but Josh had been cute and unassuming in his profile pictures and he sounded great on paper. Stable, secure. He was the lead graphic designer for a big company and worked a hybrid schedule. He was a valuable employee and was given a lot of flexibility; there was a promotion on the horizon; he'd get a big salary bump and be given his own team of designers to lead—Josh's words.

He had a lot to say about his job and accomplishments, but she wasn't sure if he knew what she did for a living, even though she had mentioned it several times. The conversation had been stilted and one-sided so far, but Shyanne was willing to chalk that up to first date nerves. But that was before he ate the last breadstick.

Now she was less interested in being nice and easy to get along with.

"Wouldn't you agree?" Josh said, leaning forward on his forearms.

Oh, Lord, he'd asked her a question. Shyanne raised her eyebrows. "I'm sorry, what?"

Josh smiled indulgently. She didn't like his smile. There was something cold about it, like it didn't reach his eyes. He was conventionally attractive, he had that going for him at least, but there was something about him that had hairs rising in alarm on the back of Shyanne's neck.

She wanted to sigh and cut the date early, but Josh was giving off vibes that indicated that particular action would not go over well.

"I read this article in the *Times*, about the resurgence of trad wives and the nuclear, *natural* family. I think it's great that women are realizing that coming back to a more traditional role is making everyone happier. Don't you agree?"

Shyanne's whole body froze; she was sure every strand of her meticulously curled hair had frozen too.

Josh was swigging his beer, like he hadn't just revealed himself to be a gigantic sexist, misogynist.

Shyanne smoothed the velvet down her thighs. "Do I look like a trad wife to you?"

Josh paused, his gentle façade slipping. "Well, I'm sure they all look...different."

Shyanne cocked her head. "I'm a board-certified doctor who owns fifty-percent of a family medicine practice. Or did you miss all that?"

The tips of Josh's ears tinged the slightest bit pink. She didn't think he had it in him to be embarrassed, but she guessed there was a first time for everything.

"Well, you know, you're not exactly young." His chest puffed out like he'd finally stumbled upon a way to win his argument. "I figure you'd need to quit if you want to have a family or a husband."

Shyanne sucked on her front teeth, a very un-trad-wife habit that usually preceded her saying something feral. She resisted, though, because she knew there was no way she'd be able to convince Josh of the error of his ways.

She dabbed her cloth napkin at the edges of her mouth before laying it on the table. "Well, that was illuminating. I wish you the best in your search for what you're looking for."

She stood, her evening wristlet swinging wildly.

"Hey, wait! You should at least pay for your half."

Shyanne laughed. It was the funniest thing he'd said all night. "Consider it a payment for wasting my time."

Josh spluttered. "What about my time?"

But Shyanne was already walking to the exit, her nude-heeled sandals, which she only ever wore with this dress, clicking across the floor.

She half expected to be followed. Adrenaline was pumping through her body, making her almost dizzy as she crossed the dark parking lot. She had her keys stuck through her fingers like claws. She made it to the safety of her car without incident, starting and locking the doors before letting out a relieved breath.

Then someone knocked on her window and she screamed, heart lurching.

Josh was at the door, making the universal sign for "roll down the window." He wasn't conventionally attractive any more in the dark.

She tugged her phone from her wristlet and typed 911 in the keypad and then held it up for Josh to see. He frowned and then said, "Please."

She could hear him faintly through the closed door, which was all he was going to get.

"No," she said, shaking the phone again. Then she tossed it in the passenger seat. If he wouldn't move, she'd just run him over. She turned her headlights on and put the car in reverse.

Josh took a large, alarmed step back, forehead creased with disappointment. She could see his mouth moving in her peripheral vision, but now he was too far away from the car for her to make out any specific words. She could just hear a vague thrum of sound. Nothing he could say now would make any lick of a difference.

She reversed out of her parking spot as quickly as she could, while still keeping an eye on Josh. She didn't actually want to hit him if it wasn't absolutely necessary.

He faded in her rearview mirror, the lone, blinking light post washing out his pale face.

Shyanne had bought her house the same year Jim had asked her to become a partner. His sudden interest in partnership was allegedly brought on by his desire to retire and spend more time with his new grandchildren. It had been two years, and Jim was still flitting around the practice with barely reduced hours and only delegating to her when he absolutely needed to.

He didn't act like a man on the verge of retirement, but that was okay with Shyanne. The salary boost was enough to keep her very comfortable and she enjoyed being swept under Jim's wing.

He was a staple in their community; their patients trusted and loved him and he was a wonderful mentor. Besides, Jim's aversion to retirement worked in her favor; she wasn't ready to carry the practice by herself, and soon, she'd need the extra free time anyway.

The house was Shyanne's dream home. A cute, three-bedroom split ranch in an established neighborhood, only minutes from the practice. It was old enough to still have some character, but not so old that all her money went towards repairs. She could make upgrades and improvements on her own timeline, and enjoyed home projects when she took time off from work. She'd already repainted the whole interior, updated the kitchen, and made one of the bedrooms into a cozy, cottagecore home office; she'd splurged on a huge, slouchy, oversized armchair where she spent most of her nights and rainy afternoons.

It was perfect. It was a book girl's wet dream. Shyanne loved the life she'd built for herself and her cat, and assholes like Josh could shove it up their butts.

Her lights were on smart plugs and she turned them on via the app on her phone as she changed into matching pajamas, tossing her date dress and heels on the floor of her closet. She'd deal with them tomorrow. Tonight, she'd wallow and lament over another bad date in a string of bad dates.

Shyanne ran a hand down her still mostly-flat stomach. Her belly had always carried a bit of roundness, so the tiny bump was barely distinguishable. It could also just be the shadows of her dimly lit bedroom. She rubbed the spot in gentle circles. She was only three months along—and according to the pregnancy book she'd ordered, she shouldn't expect to start showing for another month or two.

She snorted. Shyanne completed college, med school, and a residency. She was originally interested in obstetrics as a specialty. She knew—logically and professionally—about pregnancy. But hormones are wild. And she needed the book to comfort her, to tell her everything she was feeling (and not feeling) was completely normal. She liked books. She processed information best through reading.

Shyanne had just grabbed her ginger tea and was about to curl up in her reading chair with her book when the doorbell rang once, and then was followed by a sharp knock on the front door.

CHAPTER TWO
DEAN

The four-foot light tube smashed across Dean's back and he fell to one knee, exaggerating the pain so he could cover his face with his arm, to keep shards out of his eyes.

Don't get it wrong, it still fucking hurt, but Dean was about over this match and getting bloodied for the night.

He hated these gimmicky, hardcore house shows. He didn't mind the indie circuit—they had made his career—but every year the promoters became more and more ambitious, thinking about what kind of spectacle they could create to draw bigger crowds.

Tonight, it was a fans-bring-the-weapons match. Almost anything was on the table; kids brought wiffle ball bats stuck through with rusty nails.

Rough hands gripped his shoulders and a sweat-slick cheek pressed to his.

"You done, Akers?"

Dean knew the other man in passing—he went by the ring name Big Beef and he earned the moniker. The man was huge, almost an entire head taller than Dean, and twice as broad. He was also an agile motherfucker, light on his feet for a man his size. Dean gripped the man's biceps and they grappled for position, moving away from where the light tube had shattered.

"Let's end it," Dean said.

They separated, and Dean chopped him across the chest with most of his forearm. Big Beef stumbled for a moment before righting himself, grabbing Dean's shoulder, and flinging him into the ropes.

Dean bounced.

He could have ducked the clothesline, but that's how they'd decided to end the match.

Big Beef's massive forearm whacked him across the chest with enough force to steal his breath; his grunt was genuine. Dean was momentarily on his knees again, before Big Beef lifted him up. Dean pushed with his feet to give the lift momentum, while Big Beef controlled his fall back down to the mat.

Dean landed flat on his back with a satisfying *thwack* to the boos and cheers of the audience.

Big Beef pinned him and the ref slid into the ring to call the three count. Dean didn't struggle to kick out and extend the drama, mostly because he was afraid there was glass in his back and he didn't want to aggravate the injury.

"One"—smack—"two"—smack—"three"—smack. "And your winner!"

Big Beef let Dean go, and stood up with the ref, arms raised in victory.

"Big Beef from Sandusky, Ohio!"

Win or lose, Dean got paid just for showing up. So, he laid on his back and stared up at the fluorescent lights of the community center gym they were in. It was a far cry from sprawling domes and sixty thousand fans and expensive light shows. But Dean guessed beggars couldn't be choosers.

He used to feel something after each match; something akin to lightning zapping through his blood stream; it was pleasure, adrenaline, a high that was better than drugs.

Now, he only felt an emptiness in his chest and a dull throbbing in his back.

Dean must've been a glutton for punishment. That was the only explanation for why he'd spent his career wrecking his body and kept showing up on the doorstep of his high school girlfriend.

They hadn't dated officially since they were eighteen, but Dean couldn't help but find himself drawn into her orbit, wherever she was, like he was her moon.

He braced a hand on the frame while he waited.

He heard the patter of footsteps and then a small light on the camera lit up, like someone was checking it.

He grinned into the camera and the deadbolt clicked.

Shyanne appeared in the doorway, her mouth and brows pulled down in a frown that was comforting in a strange way. She frowned at him a lot. Her mossy green eyes darted down the street both ways.

"Expecting someone else?" Dean asked, trying to ignore the sudden, hot jealousy that stabbed him through the middle. It would serve him right that she was expecting someone else to show up at her door in the middle of the night.

Her beleaguered sigh was barely repressed. "Not at this hour. What are you doing here?"

"I need you to look at something."

Could Dean go to urgent care or the ER? He technically could. But he didn't exactly have any health insurance at the moment and he wanted to see her. It was a thin excuse at best but it was better than telling her how he really felt.

Her frown deepened, but she motioned him to come inside anyway, quickly pulling the door closed and locking it behind them.

"Let me get my kit." She padded out of the kitchen and to the hall closet, where he knew she kept a stash of first aid supplies. It unfortunately wasn't the first time he'd come to her for a quick patch job.

He pulled a chair out from the table and spun it around, sitting on it backwards and pulling his shirt over his head.

The peaceful quiet of the house was suddenly interrupted by the angry yowling of Shyanne's fat and grumpy orange cat.

The cat parked himself in the archway that separated the kitchen and living room and glared at Dean, clearly judgmental.

"Shoo, cat." Dean waved his shirt in the cat's direction but the orange menace didn't flinch.

"Don't be nasty to him." Shyanne reentered the room, her arms laden with the supplies she might need to treat him. Her eyes raked his now bare upper body.

There was no heat, though, much to Dean's disappointment. Her purview was clinical and detached.

She sat her supplies on the counter and then snapped on a pair of blue latex gloves, pushing a pair of reading glasses up her nose with her wrist.

He heard her gasp when she finally got a good look at his back. He guessed it looked worse than it felt. Dean hadn't bothered to try to catch a peek of the damage before he changed and drove over here.

"What the fuck did you do, Dean?"

He felt her clinical fingers, her blunt nails, gingerly touching different spots across his shoulder blades.

He wanted to shrug, but didn't dare move or he'd incur more of her ire.

"You did another one of those hardcore matches, didn't you," she scolded, and the cat yowled again, like he was bitching at Dean too. "What the fuck did you get hit with?"

"Light bulb," he said flatly, eyes fixed at nothing in front of him.

Shyanne cursed some more under her breath as she examined him. Her touch was soft, but still irritated the cuts, leaving a stinging pulse as she worked.

He liked coming to her house for the mere fact that it felt like a home, like someone lived here. It was cozy and homey, despite the angry feline. It smelled like Shyanne, clean like laundry right out of the dryer. His apartment was spartan and white; it looked like a rental. There was no heart, no personality. It wasn't a home. It was a place he slept when he needed to.

He hated that fucking apartment because it reminded him of everything he could have had and everything he lost.

"Nothing needs stitches, but Jesus Christ, Dean. What have I told you about those matches? Do you know how many bloodborne pathogens you can be exposed to?"

Dean quirked a smile. "Yes, Dr. Bennett. You have."

She snorted behind him and then he hissed as cold antiseptic hit his abused skin. "I'm going to put some liquid bandage over them. I think you'll live. This time."

Her tone of voice made it very clear how she felt about the subject. But that was something he already knew. Shyanne—who had always wanted to study medicine—never understood Dean's fascination with wrestling. With throwing his body around in the ring, with embracing the pain and the toll the sport takes on a body. Now, after almost two decades, Dean wasn't really sure he understood it anymore either. He'd devoted his life to a sport, an industry, that didn't love him back.

Shyanne moved back into his line of sight. She was barefoot, her toes painted the same dark green as her eyes. She wore a pair of matching lavender pajamas—purple was her favorite color—covered in small white flowers. There were cuffs at her wrists and ankles, and little lapels at her collarbones. Her coppery auburn hair was held up by one of those big claw clips, stray pieces falling around her high cheekbones.

She pulled her gloves off and tossed them in the trash can.

Shyanne's eyes narrowed as she grabbed his chin, tilting his head up. "Your lip is split."

"Is it?" Dean's tongue darted out to lick at the small break and Shyanne's gaze followed the movement. Her inspection wasn't quite so professional this time.

Her chest was level with his face and he just couldn't resist. He'd never been able to resist her. Dean brought a hand up and cupped her breast, thumb rubbing over her nipple.

"Are your tits bigger today?"

She smacked his hand away, a flush blooming over her cheeks. "Put your shirt on."

She went to clean up the medical supplies and put them away, Dean's eyes never leaving her form. Was her ass bigger too?

It'd been almost three months since they'd seen each other, but Dean had been fucking this woman for almost twenty years...he knew her body like he knew his own. She looked...fuller. Dean hoped that meant that she was happy, that work was going well and she wasn't grinding herself into the ground. In med school, there had been all-nighters and too much caffeine and hollow cheeks and protruding collarbones from skipping meals.

Dean did not put his shirt on. He shot the cat a lascivious grin and then rose to follow Shyanne down the hall.

She had just shut the hall closet door and was in the middle of turning back towards the kitchen when she spied Dean.

Her mouth opened—probably to scold him some more—but she snapped it shut when Dean pinned her to the wall with his chest pressed against hers. He closed her in with his hands on either side of her head.

Her expression was severe. He didn't like that one. He wanted her to be soft, languid. He wanted to kiss the frown away from her plump mouth. He'd kiss her and touch her until she was sighing and sated.

"Dean."

"Do you want me to go?" He pressed his body tighter to hers; pressed his quickly hardening cock against her thigh. "Tell me to go and I will."

There was a war going on in her eyes; he could see it in the way she wet her lips, sucking them into her mouth with indecision.

Dean curled a thick strand of her hair around his index finger, the movement releasing a waft of her shampoo.

She inhaled. Then he felt her warm hands skim up his sides. Goose bumps broke out all up and down his arms.

"We shouldn't."

"You say that every time."

"You're hurt."

"Then be gentle with me."

Her palms flattened on his stomach, the muscles there clenching under her touch. If she moved them just a little lower, she could slide them under the waistband of his joggers.

Her conflicted eyes were still searching his face, though.

Dean's need for her was a hungry, fierce thing that constricted his chest. He needed her. He needed to feel something other than the bone-deep, icy apathy that had been haunting him for the last few years. She was the only thing in his life that made sense anymore; she had always made sense, even if he was too much of an ass to tell her that.

He pressed his forehead to hers, closing his eyes. "Please, Shy. Don't ask me to leave." He was surprised his voice hadn't cracked.

He felt her sigh, felt her chest compress, her warm breath floating over his mouth. Her hands slid over his hips, down the back of his pants, her blunt nails digging into the meat of his ass. His balls tightened.

Still with his eyes closed, Dean moved one of his hands over to the buttons of her pajama top, starting with the one at her throat. They were easy to undo, and he felt her breathing hitch as he moved down her sternum.

Dean slipped his hand inside, cupping her swollen breast, thumb brushing over her already-hard nipple. He played with the soft flesh until she rewarded him with a breathy moan, her hips seeking his. She opened her thighs so that their pelvises could slot together; he ground his erection against her soft heat.

Dean licked a stripe up her throat, reveling in the feel of her pulse under his tongue; a frantic throbbing that echoed the pulsing of his cock.

Shyanne's hips bucked, breath catching in her throat. "Dean, don't tease me. Fuck me if you're going to fuck me."

Dean grinned against her throat. She had always been an impatient, insatiable little thing. He slid his free hand—the one not playing with her nipple—into her pajama bottoms. She wasn't wearing any underwear.

Her core was searing hot and sopping wet. He dragged fingers through her folds. "Look at you. Already dripping and I've barely touched you."

She whined, her hands rubbing over the notched muscles at his hips and stomach, pushing at his pants.

He played with her clit leisurely, alternating between rubbing the swollen bud and dipping one of his fingers inside her grasping heat.

Dean felt his pants finally slip free of his waist and a hot hand gripped his cock none too gently. He hissed, hips jerking into her touch. She wasn't gentle as she stroked him, pressing her thumb into his slit, spreading precum along the tip.

It was Dean's turn to whine against her throat, even as he fingered her. They panted in ragged tandem, breaths loud in the quiet house. Shyanne nipped at his lips and he captured her mouth in a bruising kiss. It was always a battle of wills between them, a contest of who would surrender first.

Dean jerked her pants off her ass, the material puddling at her feet. Shyanne lifted one leg, hooking it on his hip, notching his cock at her entrance. Dean sank inside with one decisive thrust, Shyanne's wet cunt parting with ease, as if welcoming him home.

They groaned simultaneously and Shyanne breathed out "Fuck" against his ear. She gripped the small of his back, his bicep, her hands careful to avoid the damage spread across his shoulder blades.

Dean wouldn't have cared, though, if she ripped him apart.

Chapter Three

Shyanne

Shyanne shouldn't have let Dean Akers stay the night.

She shouldn't have let him fuck her against the wall. Shouldn't have let him fuck her on her knees in her bed. Shouldn't have let him fall asleep tucked behind her, his cock still buried inside her, their legs tangled together.

She probably also shouldn't have fucked him raw, but they had always played fast and loose with condom usage—even though she *really* knew better—which had led to her current situation.

She was pregnant with Dean's child and hadn't told him yet and he noticed the subtle changing of her body; changes she had barely noticed.

Dean was a bad habit she kept telling herself she was going to quit and then never did.

Every time was supposed to be the last time; she was supposed to be finally moving on with her romantic life—the one facet of her life still in shambles—and finding someone who matched her lifestyle. Who was in the same stage of life as she was.

Dean was unsettled; he always had been. He followed the money and the business and he always had. He wasn't safe or steady or reliable.

She also should not have let him stay asleep while she got ready for work, but she did that too. He just looked so damn peaceful, sprawled out in her lavender sheets. The circles under his eyes were so dark, it looked like someone had pressed them there with their thumbs. Cuts from the light bulb were sprinkled across his taut shoulder blades like a constellation of stars. Thankfully, they were all shallow and superficial and none were actively bleeding; like usual, he'd heal right up and then be on his way to the next city, next event, next paycheck.

His body was a map of his life: lean, wiry muscles, more scars than she could count, and black ink.

Before she'd left, Meatloaf had jumped up on the bed and yowled at her, as if he somehow knew she had the urge to run her finger along Dean's hard jaw.

She wasn't going to touch. She just wanted to *look*.

She gave the cat a dirty scowl—as *he* was snuggling up on the pillow beside Dean's head—before packing up her work bag, her prenatal vitamins, her mobile blood pressure cuff, and her advanced maternal age-approved lunch and heading to the office.

Their practice was small and cozy and her days were usually pretty calm and routine; there weren't a lot of surprises among her regulars.

She waved at the front desk and they greeted her warmly, "Good morning, Dr. Bennett!"

She took her lunch bag to the shared breakroom and tucked it into the fridge. As she was closing the door, the medical assistant, Sam, popped her head into the doorway.

"Dr. Bennett, your nine o'clock interview is here."

Shyanne froze. Fuck. She had completely forgotten that they had interviews today for a soon-to-be-vacant medical receptionist role. She would have dressed better and thrown some makeup on. She wore her regular hot pink scrubs and purple Crocs, her hair pulled up in a semi-neat ponytail.

"Is Jim in yet?"

Sam shook her head, a bit of a nervous look on her face. "Do you want me to tell them to wait?"

Shyanne resisted the urge to run her hand over her belly; it was a nervous habit she was developing, and she hadn't told anyone at the office yet about her condition.

"No, it's fine, I'll take it. When's my first appointment?"

"Nine thirty."

Shyanne's brows rose. She was cutting it close today.

Sam grimaced. "Yeah, I know. The scheduling software is on the fritz and Hannah's freaking out."

Shyanne sighed. Their scheduling software had been lagging for a while now, but they didn't want to replace it before they hired a new medical receptionist, so they didn't have to train everyone twice. If they didn't make a hiring decision soon, they'd be short staffed and short one outdated scheduler.

Shyanne checked the time on her phone (she was not going to admit she was checking for any texts from Dean, no, she was not) and then slipped it into her back pocket.

"Okay, we can do this. Come get me at five till for the nine thirty. Smooth as butter, baby."

Sam grinned. "Smooth as butter."

Shyanne's interviewee turned out to be just as bad as her date last night. He looked good on paper, but he was haughty and she could tell he wasn't interested in the job as more than a temporary stop. She'd be hiring again in six months, judging by the way his nose crinkled when he talked about living in Cedar Creek.

She loved her hometown. She wasn't about to have someone treat their patients like shit on the bottom of a shoe.

Sam was punctual, as usual, and her nine thirty turned out to be none other than Jesse Lee Abel.

Jesse was a big man, ruggedly handsome, and had really leaned into the country lifestyle with a flannel shirt and boots. She had just seen him a couple weeks ago.

"Dr. Bennett," he greeted, his voice rumbling low in his chest like it always did.

"Not another sex injury, I hope," she teased, just to see his ears turn pink.

He smiled, and it was one of those soft, secret smiles of a man infatuated. She'd heard what happened between him and Teddy at the gym—his lip was still on the mend. There were so many witnesses, basically the whole town had heard that he was sleeping with Teddy's daughter, who was two decades his junior, but that Harper had to pull her dad off while also confessing her love.

It was all very dramatic and romantic and Sam and Hannah swooned when they reenacted the story around the office.

"Just a checkup," Jesse said, rolling up his sleeve so she could get a look at his wrist.

Shyanne pulled her gloves on and her glasses down out of her hair. "How's your range of motion? Pain?"

Jesse moved his wrist in a circle and flexed it back and forth for her. "Fine. It's all fine."

Shyanne snapped her gloves off and tossed them. "Well, it looks great. No redness or swelling. Teddy's insurance must be great if you can come in here for me to just tell you what I'm sure you already know." She crossed her legs, rolling her stool around with one foot, arms propped on her knee.

Jesse rolled his sleeve back down and buttoned it, not really looking at her. He had always been a bit of an enigma, a bit of a loner, even though girls swooned over him and gym guys worshipped him like a god. He'd caused quite the stir when he moved to town and started working at Teddy's gym. Jesse Lee was actually *famous* famous, especially in the professional wrestling circles. He had the kind of career she felt Dean was always chasing.

Jesse was positively fidgeting, which was unusual to see from a man who was usually so stoic.

"Was there something else?" she asked.

The tops of his ears turned pink. "Did you hear...uh...about the...situation at the gym?"

Shyanne snorted. "Who didn't? Brawling, Jesse, really?"

"I didn't swing first," he said indignantly. "Is it bad? What people are saying?"

"Uh, no. It's like a fairy tale. I'll never hear the end of it from my front office. Did you really come out here to ask me that? You could have put that in the group chat."

Jesse's eyes widened, clearly startled by her mention of a group chat. She did have a chat with Teddy and his young assistant in case something happened that she could handle with minimal fuss. Most of the guys didn't have decent—or any—health insurance.

"I'll add you," she teased. "So, you can just text next time."

Jesse ran a hand over his stubble. "I just don't want her to have any regrets. Choosing me, you know?"

Oh, God, had he come to her for relationship advice? Was he aware of the dismal state of her love life? The man at home? The conflicted feeling in her gut? The hope he'd leave quietly or the even more absurd hope that he'd stay?

Shyanne gave him what she hoped was an encouraging, hopeful smile. "She's lucky to have you, Jesse."

By the end of her workday, Shyanne had almost—*almost*—forgotten about the naked man she'd left in her bed.

She'd spent the day checking her phone, which was out of character for her, and frowned each time there wasn't a missed call or a new text message. She had plenty of texts from her cousin's group chat, more matches from her dating apps (she *really* needed to deactivate her profile), but nothing from Dean.

Not a *hi, hello, goodbye, see ya later,* or *fuck you.*

If he was gone, he was gone, and she could keep moving on with her life. She tossed her phone into her bag with more force than necessary and followed Sam and Hannah out the front door, while Sam locked up.

The girls chatted happily as they all walked to the parking lot.

"Do you wanna come?"

Shyanne had to pause in the process of unlocking her car door because the question was clearly directed at her and she hadn't really been paying attention to the details of their conversation.

"Come where?"

"Drinking. End o' Road."

Shyanne frowned. "It's a Tuesday."

Both girls gave her looks that clearly said, *And your point is?*

Oh, to be in her twenties again. Shyanne didn't mind a little drink here or there, but all she was good for anymore was a glass of wine and then she'd be out like a light. She also tried not to make it a habit of drinking with the people she ran payroll for.

"August is working tonight," Sam added, and Hannah's cheeks turned red.

Shyanne smiled. August was sweet—probably too sweet for his own good—and half the town had a crush on him. "No, thanks. You have fun, though."

"See you in the morning!" They waved, both piling into Sam's car.

Shyanne checked her phone one more time. Nothing.

She was used to coming home to an empty house, with Meatloaf howling for pets and his dinner. Shyanne was surprised when she opened the front door to find neither of those things were true.

Her house was not empty.

And Meat was not howling because he was winding through Dean's ankles as he stood at the stove.

Her heart thumped dully in her chest.

Shyanne stood in the entrance, dazed.

Dean was still here, in her house. He hadn't left.

Dean had changed. He was in tight black joggers, wool socks, and a maroon V-neck tee that was tight around his biceps and showed off the tattoos on his throat and chest.

He looked up, spied Shyanne, and gave her one of his signature dazzling smiles—the kind that used to make her swoon in her teens—like this was the most natural occurrence in the world.

Still slightly dazed, Shyanne hung up her keys, toed off her Crocs and put them neatly on the hall tree, set her lunch bag on the counter.

"You're still here," she said, stating the obvious.

"I am," he replied, eyes going back to what he was working on. It looked like some kind of pasta.

It was odd to see Dean doing something so domesticated.

Shyanne leaned a hip against the counter. "What are you making?"

"Chicken carbonara."

Chicken carbonara. It had been her favorite dish at an old Italian place they used to go to multiple times a week. Coincidence? "I didn't know you knew how to cook."

He flashed her another grin, one that sent a skitter down her spine. "A man can learn how to do new things."

She snorted.

"Plus, I know that it's your favorite."

Well, that at least answered one question.

Dean stirred, and dashed salt and pepper over his dish. He shouldn't look so fucking hot in the kitchen, but Dean looked hot doing about everything. The defined muscles in his hands and forearms flexed deliciously as he moved.

She felt her skin grow hot. She was hungry for pasta and Dean, her stomach rumbling even as her pussy clenched uncomfortably.

No. Why was he still here? He didn't stay multiple nights, he didn't make dinner for her, he didn't entertain her cat. He was always gone to the next show or gig or temporary placement. He didn't *linger*.

And now how was she supposed to kick him out after he cooked her favorite comfort food?

Shyanne was still having her silent deliberation when Dean tapped his spoon against the lip of the pan, turning the heat down.

"Why don't you go get cleaned up? This only has a few more minutes and then it'll be ready."

And then would he leave? If she ate his dinner?

Shyanne nodded, and mouthed, "Traitor" at Meatloaf as she passed him, sitting docilely at Dean's feet.

She took a quick shower, brushed her hair and put it in a messy braid, and pulled on a pair of yoga pants and a baggy crew neck sweater. Despite Dean seeing her pajamas last night—and many nights before that—she felt going right into her pajamas would send the wrong message.

Dean had set the table—two settings. He'd included small bowls of Cesar salad, glasses of water, and had even found the wineglasses.

He hadn't poured anything yet; he was holding the wine bottle as she re-entered the kitchen and showed her the label.

"How much?"

"Oh, no, sweet wine gives me headaches." It was the best excuse she could come up with in the moment that wasn't the truth.

Dean chuckled as he poured the fruity wine into just one of the glasses. "You used to not be so discerning."

Shyanne sat down, examining the lightly steaming pile of pasta before her. Much to her chagrin, it looked and smelled amazing, perfectly creamy. "Yeah, well, some of us grow up, Dean."

It was a cheap shot, she knew that, but took it anyway. Dean had her off guard, with his fucking pasta and quips about their history together.

If Dean took offense to her tone, he didn't show it. He just sat down across from her, at her small farmhouse table, and sipped his wine. Dean wasn't a wine guy; she only knew him to drink beer or bourbon. And yet, here he was, drinking wine and cooking dinner.

They ate in silence for a few minutes and Shyanne couldn't decide if it was a comfortable one.

"So," he said finally, "better or worse than Buca's?"

"It's really good, Dean." Maybe it was nostalgia, maybe it was just her pregnancy hormones, but the pasta was mouth-wateringly good, each bite melting in her mouth.

Dean just made a pleased humming sound before going back to his own plate.

Shyanne groped around for something else to say. They were good in the bedroom—too fucking good—but it had been a long time since they did anything like this. Just dinner, just a meal, together.

"How's your back feeling?"

He smirked. "I'm good, doc. You do a hell of a patch job."

Shyanne wanted to say more, wanted to ask him when enough was enough, when he was going to stop putting his body through hell for a dream that was never going to materialize.

But they had had that conversation, or some variation of it, many times throughout the years and it always ended the same way.

She couldn't seem to stop the sigh that escaped her lips.

Dean caught it. "What's wrong?"

Shyanne wanted to laugh, but knew that it would be hysterical. What wasn't wrong, that was the real question. But Dean didn't know about the little secret she carried—literally. She knew she needed to tell him, probably sooner rather than later, but she was kind of hoping to delay what was sure to be a horrible conversation for as long as possible.

"Shy, are you listening to me? I asked you what's wrong." Dean's voice was sharp and firm and sent a shiver down her limbs. Damn fucking pregnancy hormones.

Apparently, she was just going to oscillate between hungry and horny.

"I'm just...tired, Dean. I work all day and I just want to come home. And dinner was nice but now there are all these dishes and..." Shyanne trailed off, not really sure where she was going. She pressed the heels of her hands to her eyes; there was a tightness forming behind her eyes, a throb in her temples. Fuck. Was she going to cry now?

"Hey, hey." There were suddenly warm palms sliding up and down her thighs in slow, soothing strokes. "Don't cry, Shy. I'll take care of the dishes. And wipe the counters. And take the trash out and replace the bag."

Shyanne let out a sound that was somewhere between a choked laugh and a sob. She pressed harder against her eyes until she saw bright lights, then she let go.

Dean was down on his knees in front of her, strong hands stroking her thighs and then her hips, fingers digging pleasantly into her skin, her tight muscles.

It was more than just the hormones, Shyanne knew that. They just brought every wound, every hurt, closer to the surface and made her feel everything much more keenly.

It hurt because, once upon a time, she had wanted this—wanted it with him. The home, the dinner, the cat, the easy domesticity, their baby on the way.

She had wanted it, and he didn't, and that wound was long and deep and bleeding in her chest.

Dean's hands kept up their gentle but firm massage, and against her better judgement, Shyanne could feel some of the tension seep from her body. He always did have the best hands, strong and wide, with lithe fingers that were more suited for a musician than an athlete.

And, oh, the things those fingers could do, could make her feel.

She felt his warm lips press a kiss to her forehead. Shyanne grabbed his head, shaved hair prickly under her fingertips, and crashed her lips to his. Dean's mouth opened hungrily under the kiss, his hands slipping up her sweater and into the waistband of her yoga pants. She gasped at the feel of his warm hands on her stomach.

Dean broke the kiss, grinning at her as he tugged at her pants, his intention clear. Shyanne lifted her hips so he could pull her pants and underwear down her legs until they tangled in her ankles. He rubbed his palms up her calves, her knees, her thighs, pressing her legs open.

"Let me see my pussy, Shy."

Shyanne's breath shuddered out of her as she spread her legs wider, scooting down in the chair and gripping the edge of the table with one hand. "I don't know if it's yours," she retorted, voice breathy anyway.

His coffee-brown eyes darkened as he gazed at that hot spot between her legs. The more he looked, the harder it was to breathe. His hands slid to the soft insides of her thighs. "It's always been mine. Do you want me to show you?" His thumbs stroked across her lightly thatched mound.

Shyanne knew it was just sex talk, but the way he purred *mine* twisted up her insides and set her cunt to throbbing in time with her pulse.

"Just look how wet you're getting for me and I'm just looking. Wet and grasping, Shyanne."

Shyanne moaned, arching her back in the hopes of putting her aching core closer to his mouth.

Dean made a deep, appreciative humming sound in the back of his throat. His thumbs stroked her, moving closer to her center, opening her up layer by layer. She could feel his fingers slipping over her wet flesh until they met at her clit.

Her hips bucked at the touch. "Dean, fuck."

He wet a thumb in her cunt, brushing it softly back and forth over her aching clit. The pressure was just enough to send spasms through her belly, pleasure building at a leisurely pace. It was nice, but it wasn't going to get her anywhere.

"Dean," she pleaded, hips squirming, seeking, as he just petted and teased her.

"I want to hear you say it."

"Say what?" Her voice was a harsh whisper. Whatever he wanted, she was ready to give him in this moment.

"I want to hear you say this pussy is mine." His hot breath ghosted over the sensitive skin of her inner thighs.

She still had enough wits about her to chafe at the directive. But what was the harm of giving him what he wanted?

"It's yours," she all but growled.

He traced a finger down her slit. "Say it all, Shyanne."

She squirmed, legs quaking, but they were held open by Dean's firm shoulders. The finger stroked, never quite penetrating her in any meaningful way.

"My pussy is yours, Dean."

He speared her with the digit and her breath hitched, hips bucking, cunt sucking. "See? That wasn't so hard, now, was it?" His voice was muffled against her thigh.

Shyanne didn't have enough rational thought left to agree or disagree with him; she didn't care. The only thing she cared about anymore was the feel of his fingers, the scrape of stubble against her thigh, the orgasm curling in her center.

He stroked the inside of her and pumped a few times before adding another finger. Shyanne bore down on his hand, trying to increase the pressure, the sensation, her nails digging into the top of the table.

She felt breath over her swollen clit and then his mouth was there, his tongue.

"Fuck." She gave up her grip on the table and grabbed his head instead, pressing him deeper into her cunt. "Fuck, fuck, fuck," she chanted.

Dean's laugh rumbled against her overheated flesh. And then he latched his mouth over her clit, sucking it, as he simultaneously jammed another finger inside her.

Shyanne broke, the orgasm cresting over her in a series of tiny waves, causing her lashes to flutter and her thighs to shake in the aftermath. Was Dean still breathing? She should probably let his head go and check.

She ran a palm over his head and down the back of his neck.

Dean kissed his way from her core, down her thigh, and to her knee, leaving a trail of wetness behind.

"You always were my favorite dessert, Tater."

Shyanne's peaceful afterglow bubble shattered at the childhood nickname. Dean gave her the name their freshman year of high school because she always asked for extra mashed potatoes at lunch. He was the only person in the world to ever call her that.

Why did he have to bring that up now, at this moment? Another reminder of everything they'd had before.

She wriggled, suddenly uncomfortable bare in the kitchen with her pants and underwear around her ankles.

Dean sat back on his heels, giving her an odd, unreadable look, like he knew the nickname had made her uncomfortable but wasn't quite sure why. After all, it was harmless. Just a name.

"I'm going to...lie down." She felt a little guilty just getting up from the table and leaving, but he had said he'd do the dishes.

Dean snagged her wrist. "Are you okay?"

She tugged herself free, trying to avoid rubbing her stomach self-consciously. "Yeah, I'm just going...to make some tea and then go to bed. It helps me sleep."

They did a weird, strange, silent dance in the kitchen, avoiding touching each other even though he'd just been face-deep in her vagina. Shyanne bustled around, making her ginger tea, while Dean cleared the table and put away leftovers like he lived here.

She held the warm mug between her palms, blowing gently on the steam. "It's late, Dean."

He wiped his hands on a dish towel and then folded it over the sink. "I know. I'll—"

"Stay," she blurted, before she could convince herself it was a bad idea. Her guilt nagged at her like a bad hangnail. "I'm not going to kick you out after that dinner and dessert." She smiled at him.

Dean sidled up to her, pecking her cheek and rubbing a palm over her ass, careful not to jostle her arms. "Let's get you tucked in, then."

CHAPTER FOUR

DEAN

Dean watched Shyanne get ready for work.

She paired her hot pink scrubs with a pair of tall floral socks, brushing dry shampoo through her hair and then pulling it up into a neat ponytail. She tamed the flyaways with a few bobby pins and hair spray. She didn't use any perfume, but rubbed unscented lotion on her hands at the end of her routine.

"What?" She paused in the bathroom doorway to turn off the mounted wall fan and lights.

Dean shrugged. "Just watching." She narrowed her eyes at him but he only grinned. "I enjoy the view."

She snorted, shooing him away from the bed so that she could straighten the decorative pillows and knitted throw blanket across the bottom. He noticed that she didn't shoo away the orange menace, who had already made a divot in one of the pillows. She scratched behind his ears, and the cat arched up into her touch, with a *look* at Dean.

Dean didn't think animals could look smug, but the fat cat certainly did.

"Should I expect to see you tonight?" She was still petting the cat, his tail furling around her hand.

Dean's hand brushed over Shyanne's hip, enjoying the way her body reacted, even as she had her face schooled in cool neutrality. She was hiding something, but Dean couldn't fathom what the fuck it could be.

"You can, if you want." He didn't have any jobs booked for the foreseeable future, although he was hesitant to admit that to Shyanne—she'd just have something to say about it.

She gave the cat one more pat and then pulled away, very business-like. "I have plans tonight. So, I'll just see you around, okay."

Dean wanted to cringe. This was like the world's worst morning-after walk. He followed her to the front door as she gathered her things for work.

"I'm thinking of checking out that new gym Teddy Myles opened."

Shyanne swung her coat on. "You should. Jesse Lee Abel coaches there now."

Of course, Dean knew what Jesse Lee was up to. His retirement plans had been a big deal. Most people assumed he would go to coaching collegiate wrestling, so the fact that he chose to stay in the business was a surprise to most.

"Maybe you could talk to Teddy about coaching." There was a hopeful tilt to her brows, like it was just that easy.

Dean knew Teddy from the indie circuit. Their careers had taken similar trajectories, but Teddy had enough status and connections to fund opening his gym. What did Dean have?

He didn't feel like starting a fight so he just said, "Maybe."

Shyanne just didn't understand.

She'd gotten her dreams, so why couldn't he still have his? Okay, so he was a little old to still be breaking his back for the small companies and the hardcore shows. Guys didn't usually get to make their big debuts while pushing forty—it was rare, but not impossible.

Dean drummed his fingers on the steering wheel of his old, rusted-up, single cab truck that rattled when the weather got too cold. Fuck. Teddy's gym was beautiful.

His original plan was to go in, say hello, and maybe get in a nice workout.

But Dean wasn't so sure he could stand around in a room full of guys who had what he didn't and act like he was okay with that.

Dean pulled his phone out and started sending out messages to contacts and promoters. He needed to book his next gig, and quickly.

Nothing happened, but then his phone rang. It was Nate, the promoter for the western branch of Tennessee's IWA.

"Nate, what's up, man?"

"Deanie," Nate greeted, the nickname making Dean grind his molars together.

"Got anything for me?"

Nate was hollering at someone in the background; probably his nephew, who was part-owner of the promotion and liked to do illegal moves during his matches. Dean waited.

"Yeah, man, you want in on Turkey Terror? We could use a few more matches."

It would not be Dean's first Turkey Terror—a particularly bloody hardcore match that they hosted every year on Thanksgiving.

Dean rubbed at the center of his forehead. "Don't you have anything that's not hardcore?" The small cuts on his shoulders still stung.

"Uh, not really. It's what the audience wants, man. They yearn for the blood." Nate laughed, but Dean didn't join him.

A quick rap on the window startled him. Teddy Myles was at his door.

"Uh, yeah, Nate, I'll let you know."

Then he hung up the phone and grabbed the crank on the door to roll the window down.

Teddy smiled big and laughed; he always was a jovial man. "I thought I recognized you. What are you doin' lurking in the parking lot?"

Well, shit fuck.

"Oh, I was just passing through and wanted to see the new gym."

Teddy beamed, his cheeks reddening with pride. "Pretty, isn't she?" He asked the question like he was showing off a woman instead of a building.

"I can't say she's not," Dean agreed.

Teddy leaned his thick forearms on the window, like he was settling in for a long talk instead of just coming out to admonish Dean for being a creep in his parking lot.

"Don't see you around here much, huh."

Where was this conversation going? "Nah, I'm on the road a lot. You know how the indie shows go."

Teddy nodded sagely. "That I do. Hey, I'm thinking of putting together a small showcase for the gym. Just something fun for the young guys. You interested?"

"Am I going to have to lose?"

Teddy laughed and clapped him on the shoulder. "I'll pay you well if you do. Give the kids some time in the limelight."

"You've got a deal." Beggars couldn't be choosers, after all. And Teddy's showcase sounded more appealing than getting himself bloodied up at another Turkey Terror.

Teddy slipped him a glossy, embossed business card. "Send my assistant your details, okay? She'll get you set up."

Dean watched Teddy's back as he walked back to the front doors. He ran the pad of his thumb over the shiny card, the raised lettering.

Then he opened a new text thread for Raleigh French.

CHAPTER FIVE
SHYANNE

Shyanne technically didn't have any plans after work until she texted her cousins.

> SOS

> I need a cousin date immediately

Chandler

> REALLY

> What happened?

Micah

> Does 8 work? I have a job, Shyyyy

The girls, Chandler and Micah, were her uncle's kids from two different moms. They were close in age, barely a year apart, which led to the biggest scandal in Bennett family history. Her uncle and his relationships with both moms were still the leading source of family gossip. It was probably a miracle that they all had the relationship they did.

They met at Drake's, which was the most central location for everyone since it was close to both highways. Shyanne loved their drinks and sushi, neither of which she could currently have, and their tater tots, but thinking about tater tots made her think about Dean calling her Tater.

She liked potatoes in all forms, okay?

Shyanne picked at the turkey avocado melt on her plate.

"So," Chandler said, popping a piece of her spicy tuna roll into her mouth, delicately avoiding smearing her hot pink lipstick. "What's the emergency?"

Shyanne was surprised the girls let her get through their appetizer and ordered their entrees before asking.

She smoothed the napkin across her thighs. She might as well just get this over with. It was the reason she'd sent out a distress signal. "I'm pregnant."

Micah choked and Chandler's sushi roll fell off her chopsticks as she paused with the next bite almost to her mouth.

Micah gulped down a drink. Shyanne gave them a moment to absorb this new information.

They were both giving her identical flabbergasted looks. They were both blonde, but Chandler's hair was long and still her natural color, while Micah had a dramatic short pixie that she dyed platinum.

Micah recovered first. "Okay, so are we, like, happy about this? Or do we need to drive you to the clinic?"

"Or," Chandler interjected, "do we need to break some-one's knee caps?" She sounded worryingly excited about that prospect.

Shyanne shook her head with a small smile. She loved these girls and the way they immediately rallied for her, no questions asked.

She had considered an abortion as soon as she realized she was pregnant; it was her first thought. She had a friend from med school who worked at a clinic. But she had been researching IVF and artificial insemination already... She had a list of fertility doctors and baby names saved side by side in her phone.

Shyanne wanted this baby...even if it was *his* baby.

But getting accidentally pregnant was a far cry from getting purposely pregnant and Dean was an added complication that she hadn't planned on.

"No. I...want the baby." For the first time, she allowed herself to rub a hand over the barely-there bump of her stomach.

Chandler squealed, clapping her hands together. "We're having a baby!"

Micah smiled but then her brows furrowed. "Who's the baby daddy?"

Shyanne felt her face heat. "Um, well, it's Dean."

Chandler gasped and Micah rolled her eyes dramatically. "I thought you weren't fucking him anymore. It was supposed to be your New Year's Resolution."

"They're obviously meant to be." Chandler sighed, her large, extended lashes fluttering. If she were animated, she would have hearts in her eyes right now. Chandler had always been the more optimistic of the two. "What did he say?"

"I haven't told him yet." Shyanne dunked a tater tot in ketchup to avoid looking at them both. "That's kind of the problem."

"You can text him," Micah offered.

Chandler gasped, affronted. "You can't text him news like that!"

Micah grimaced, poking her straw in her Coke Zero. "Why the hell not? It's not like he's her boyfriend."

Shyanne wanted to curl up in a hole and never emerge. It was borderline embarrassing at her age to hear Micah refer to Dean as not-her-boyfriend. But her assessment was unfortunately correct.

What was Dean to her? Perpetual fuck buddy?

"You are gonna tell him, right?"

"Of course, I am going to tell him. I just...haven't had the right opportunity."

"Too busy with his dick in your mouth?" Micah grinned ferally over the table at her, eyebrows wiggling suggestively. Chandler punched her in the shoulder as their teenage server passed by and flushed.

"It seems to be what we do best." Shyanne wanted to sigh, but focused on her food instead. If they were having sex, they weren't arguing. When was the last time they had a real conversation? Shyanne didn't even know how long he was in town for or where he was going next. She'd stopped asking a long time ago because the answer was just frustrating.

"Wait, I thought you were finally actually dating other people. Didn't we make you a profile, like, months ago?"

"Yeah, about that." Shyanne put her phone face up on the table and Chandler snatched it before Micah could. "I had a date a couple days ago but *that's* not going to go anywhere."

Chandler was scrolling. "Was that this Josh guy who keeps messaging you on the app?"

Shyanne grimaced. Part of her tried-and-true dating code was not to give out her phone number until after the first date. It had saved her a lot of time and hassle; she only had to worry about blocking guys on the app. She hadn't checked the app since Dean showed up on her porch.

"Lemme see." Micah leaned over Chandler's shoulder. "Oh, he's groveling, Shy."

"Oh, ick, he called you a trad wife?" Chandler's delicate nose scrunched up.

Shyanne sipped her lemon water. "He did, unfortunately, bring up the topic of trad wives."

"Tell him to suck a dick," Micah said, pointing at the screen, which Chandler was holding out of her reach.

Shyanne snorted as the girls squabbled. She couldn't decide if it was her best idea or if it was her worst idea to put the two of them in charge of her dating life. It was probably a futile and short-lived endeavor anyway. She very much doubted she'd have many matches once she visibly started to show.

Chandler gasped and Micah squealed and Shyanne's phone was dropped on the top of the table, like it had suddenly sprouted teeth.

"That was information I did not need to be privy to."

Micah made exaggerated vomiting noises and facial expressions.

"What?" Shyanne grabbed the phone, mildly panicking that one of her matches had sent an unsolicited dick pic as they were wont to do.

But it was worse.

There was a text message from Dean...a raunchy one.

> I'm hard just thinking about you spread out for me in the kitchen chair. I can still smell your sweet pussy on my fingers.

Shyanne felt her face flush with unbidden heat. She could only stare at the phone in her hand.

"Well?" Micah. "What are you going to say back to that?"

"That"—Shyanne turned the screen off—"is none of your business."

Shyanne came home to a dark and empty house. Meatloaf wasn't even yowling at the door, but she filled his bowl up anyway.

She put her stuff down and toed her Crocs off at the door, an uncomfortable tingling sensation skittering up her limbs.

Her house wasn't any quieter or darker than it usually was but she held her breath as she stepped into the dark hallway.

A hand clamped down on the back of her neck, the other across her mouth, and she was shoved face first into the wall. Rough, but not rough enough for her body to slam against the wall. The force at her back was hard, solid, unyielding.

Shyanne's palms spread flat, her heartbeat slamming against her chest, breath hitching, a hot spark of arousal stabbing through her belly.

His hot breath ghosted over the back of her neck; she could feel his lips and teeth on the sensitive skin of her throat, the space between her throat and shoulder. She recognized his familiar scent, the calluses from weightlifting on his rough hands.

"Don't make a sound, pretty girl. Can you do that for me?" Dean's voice was a low, hungry rasp.

Shyanne nodded furiously, frantic to relieve the ache in her breasts, between her legs. She would do as he demanded because he demanded it and that was her role in this moment.

Dean's fingers traced the outline of her lips with his fingers, pressing them in her mouth, against her tongue. "You remember your safe word?"

She nodded, still silent. It had been the same since they first started experimenting with kink in college. She almost smiled at the memory, but Dean's fingers in her mouth prevented the movement. It had taken so long to convince him that yes, it was okay if he tied her up. Yes, it was okay that he slapped her ass and pulled her hair and left marks on her skin. Yes, there were certain scenarios where she could cry and scream and beg him to stop and there was nothing wrong if they both enjoyed that.

Even as she thought it, she felt his teeth again in the muscle of her shoulder, a gentle bite that promised so much more. Shyanne sucked on his fingers and pushed her ass back against his quickly hardening erection.

Dean laughed, low in his throat. "Such a desperate girl. Desperate to please. Get my fingers nice and wet." He swirled them in her mouth and Shyanne sucked and licked like they were his cock, until saliva dripped from the corners of her mouth.

He pulled his fingers free with a slight pop and Shyanne suppressed a groan. His hand slid down her pants and she widened her thighs to give him better access. The wet fingers slid through her cheeks, skimming her hole, before slipping across her cunt.

Dean didn't need her saliva. She was weeping for him already. As soon as she felt his heady presence in the darkness.

He played leisurely with her folds, spreading her, slipping his fingers in and out of her, brushing against her clit but not applying any pressure.

She knew this game.

He'd commanded her to be silent and now he was going to try to break her.

Shyanne squirmed in his hold, pressing her hard nipples into the wall, determined to create some kind of friction.

Dean made a *tsking* sound, still playing with her, one of his fingers dipping in and out of her entrance.

Shyanne bit down on her bottom lip to keep her sounds to herself. Dean's hot breath was on the shell of her ear, his voice barely a whisper. "So fucking pretty when you get so wild to come, Shyanne. Careful, don't make any sounds, baby. You know what happens when you misbehave." His teeth grabbed on to her lobe and she shuddered but remained silent.

She knew what would happen. Dean would edge her to within an inch of her life. He wouldn't let her come.

"That's my good girl," he growled, fingers rubbing hard circles against her clit.

Shyanne's knees were shaking, stomach tightening as the beginning of an orgasm finally started to build in her core. She pressed her forehead against the wall, breathing ragged but still silent. It was a battle, a challenge, issued by the man in control of her release. And she would not fail. Shyanne did not fail.

"That's it, precious girl. Keep soaking my fingers. Are you going to come from just a bit of clit play?" Dean's filthy words rasped like a physical touch against her skin. She felt the head of his cock press against her skin.

Shyanne groaned.

Fuck.

Dean's smile stretched across the back of her neck. His fingers were suddenly gone. Shyanne huffed in frustration. "Dean, please."

One hand tightened on her throat, the other digging into her hip. "You know I like you begging, but that's not what I asked you to do."

Dean snapped his hips, burying his cock inside her as deep as he could from this position. Shyanne gasped and her aching cunt clenched around the intrusion. But this wasn't for her.

Dean would take his own pleasure, use her body deliciously, until she was strung out, gasping and begging, her head full of wonderful fuzzy white noise.

His thrusts were quick, brutish, his flesh slapping against her, his grunting breath on her neck.

These days, Shyanne preferred the rough, quick sex with Dean. Anything too soft would bring certain feelings rushing back in and she didn't have any more room in her life for feelings for Dean. In college, whenever they both had a few days off, they would spend hours tangled up in bed together, alternating between sleeping and fucking and eating, like they'd never get the chance again.

Shyanne's cunt spasmed around Dean's cock, even though this wasn't supposed to be about her anymore.

Dean grunted and pulled out, hand pressing down on her shoulder, a silent order to get on her knees.

"You don't get to come until I say so."

Shyanne slid to the floor, turning her body towards his, hands skimming down his lean flanks. He fisted her ponytail, using his hold on her hair to tip her head back. Dean shoved into her mouth, and the pace he set was punishing. Shyanne's fingers dug into his hips to hold herself steady as he fucked her mouth. She relaxed her jaw and breathed through her nose, tears welling at the corners of her eyes.

He was rough, but Shyanne noted the way his hand rested on the back of her head to keep her from smacking into the wall. How he'd slow or change his pace each time she gagged. The way his dark eyes held hers, nostrils flaring, jaw tensing.

He smelled like his soap—Irish Spring—the hair at his groin tickling her nose with every thrust. She held on to his powerful thighs, feeling the muscles flex under her palms.

The pad of his thumb was gentle as he rubbed it across the soft skin under her eye. "You've always looked so pretty with my cock in your mouth." His words were soft, softer than his previous dirty talk, like this observation was something of importance, something true and real that he needed to say.

Dean's body tensed and shook before he came, his eyes glazing over. "Fuck," he ground out, shooting into her mouth, coating the back of her throat.

Shyanne tried to swallow it all down, but his spend overflowed her mouth. Dean ran his fingers through the mess, spreading cum over her lips and cheeks. She licked his thumb.

"Leave it," he rasped. "I like seeing you covered in my cum."

"You better not get any in my hair." She grinned up at him.

His lips twitched, like he was trying to restrain his own grin. "I don't think I said you could make any sound yet."

She nipped at the soft skin of his abdomen. "I guess you'll just have to start all over." Her pussy clenched at the thought. Her panties were drenched, so wet they clung to her sensitive skin.

Dean shook his head, the smile ghosting his lips. And then he did.

Several more orgasms later, they lay twined together in Shyanne's bed, slick skin stuck together. Shyanne's head rested on Dean's shoulder, one finger tracing the tattoos that snaked across his chest. He stroked her hair and the feeling was so nice, her eyelashes fluttered. She could fall asleep like this, curled against his body, feeling sated and safe. Like she wouldn't wake up and Dean would be gone again.

His thumb traced the shell of her ear. "How were the cousins?"

"They send their regards."

"Still on the Dean hate train?"

"Toot toot."

His laugh rumbled through his chest, vibrating her head. "Some things never change." He tugged on a strand of her hair. "Hey, I think I'm going to be around for a while longer. Teddy invited me to a showcase at his gym. I was thinking you could come, if you wanted."

His voice was deceptively casual, but Shyanne knew it was a sore spot—one of many—between them. She never used to miss a match, at least when they were local, but she hadn't watched him wrestle in almost ten years.

She kept rubbing circles on his pectoral, feeling goose bumps rise on his skin. "Yeah, I can try...you know, if I'm free."

He didn't respond, but she felt him nod and then press a kiss to the top of her head.

CHAPTER SIX
DEAN

Teddy's daughter was apparently some kind of big deal on the internet, and she had managed to bring enough attention to the gym to sell out their showcase. Harper Myles was kind of hard to miss. She had bright orange hair and was flitting around the place with a tripod, two cell phones, and a digital camera.

Dean didn't know what being a big deal online meant anymore; social media had lost him after Facebook. Maybe he could blame his floundering career on that and move on with his life.

The gym was packed with people.

He had to admit—only to himself and not to Teddy—that he was impressed. There were food trucks outside in the expansive parking lot; they had local news crews on site; the area surrounding the ring was surrounded by chairs and a few rented bleachers.

The performers were out back, several covered tents serving as impromptu locker rooms. They would enter through the single back door at the rear of the center. The back walls were mostly large glass windows, so they could see the people milling around inside.

Dean didn't know a lot of the other performers; they were mostly all fresh-faced, bright-eyed, unjaded young kids. One of the guys, August, had apparently been booked for OVW, which was causing quite a stir backstage. Guys were thumping the guy Dean assumed was August on the back and shoulders, while he grinned sheepishly, face a glaring red.

He'd spotted Jesse Lee when he'd arrived; he apparently wasn't participating in the showcase. Jesse Lee stood ringside with his big arms crossed, an aggrieved expression on his face, like he'd rather be anywhere but here right now. But that could just be what Jesse's face usually looked like. His sharp gaze followed Harper around the room, narrowing if anyone else dared to stop and talk to her, especially any half-naked performers.

Dean scrubbed a hand across his jaw. He'd had the thought briefly, that maybe he could talk to Jesse after the showcase about coaching and training, to see if maybe he needed a hand at the gym. But to what end? Was that really what Dean wanted? To beg for favors from people in the industry who he barely knew?

It was bad enough that Teddy took pity on him and invited him to the showcase—as the oldest performer, he was sure. Is that what he wanted, after all this time, everything he'd sacrifice? To finally give it up? Land back in the town he grew up in?

But Shyanne's here, a traitorous part of his brain whispered. That voice was getting harder and harder to ignore, especially when she slept curled up against his side like that's where she was supposed to be.

Dean flexed his arms, the muscles already complaining. He was trying not to watch the crowd, but couldn't help but keep an eye out for a certain tall, coppery-haired woman.

Shyanne hadn't said no, but she also hadn't really said yes to showing up tonight. The thought of her not showing up curdled his insides.

The back door suddenly slammed open and Dean retreated from the post he'd taken up next to the glass.

Teddy strode out, his spunky executive assistant trailing behind him with a radio and a clipboard. The man was dressed in nice black slacks, a loose black shirt, and shiny black shoes, the clean-cut outfit a far cry from the wild and flamboyant outfits of his youth. Honestly, Dean kind of missed the neon fringe and bedazzled vests.

Teddy clapped his hands together, his weathered face lit with a familiar kind of joy—joy for the game, joy for their industry—a joy that was infectious. He was renowned for his pep talks.

"We've got a full house, ladies and gentlemen. Let's not let them down and embarrass me in front of the local news and the internet. Make it look pretty."

The executive assistant—who Dean had only talked to once, to arrange for his participation tonight—named after a state capital, Raleigh, flipped her long brown hair and winked. Dean looked around, almost one hundred percent sure that it was not directed at him, to find a group of other guys tittering like teenagers.

Dean liked the spunky Raleigh; she reminded him of a young Shyanne. And there he was, thinking of her again, when his mind should be on the match.

The first match was a fifteen-man battle royale. Dean would be the tenth man to enter the ring. He was not slated to win the royale—that was one of Teddy's guys—but he'd been given enough leeway to hang in the match for a decent amount of time and, as Teddy put it, make it pretty.

There was a commotion beyond the glass: the lights started flashing, he heard the echo of music, and then a booming voice on a mic.

The younger guys crowded around, peeking over and around each other to catch a glimpse of Teddy's opener. They were excited.

Dean distinctly remembered the feeling from his first few official showings. It was like falling in love—a startling, swooping, nauseous rolling of the stomach. Sweaty palms, spasming muscles. He remembered when the sweat used to just roll down his back before he even started moving. His heart used to thump so fast sometimes he couldn't breathe.

But that was years and years ago and now, standing among the others, waiting for his name and entrance music, he might as well have been standing in line for his regular coffee order. Just another day at the office.

So, Dean waited. He itched for pockets to slide his hands into, but his black leggings didn't come with any. He was in his usual outfit—black leggings, boots, black wraps on his hands, and a grunge band T-shirt that was split up both sides, ready to be ripped off for dramatic effect.

Dean fiddled with the wraps on his hands, listening to the muffled chaos of the crowd. They were a lively bunch tonight; he could hear the cheers and boos even through the proofed glass.

The ninth guy entered the gym, the noise from the crowd crescendoing as the door swung open and shut, and Dean only had two minutes left to wait.

Finally, he heard the muffled opening notes of his entrance music—the classic "I Stand Alone" from Godsmack—and Dean entered the gym, head held down and affecting the casual swagger that was part of his bad boy brand. He didn't smile or charm or flirt with the crowd; he scowled, attention focused solely on his target: the ring.

With a powerful thrust of his legs, Dean leapt onto the apron, grabbing the top rope with one hand. One of the guys was being flung towards the rope. Dean pulled the top rope down, sending him tumbling over the edge, much to the displeasure of the crowd. He must have been popular, judging by the way they booed.

Dean climbed the turnbuckles, until he was standing on the top rope, knees slightly bent to catch his balance before his first move.

He only needed to wait about thirty seconds before Ben—the guy he was performing the move against—moved into the right position.

From his new vantage point, Dean had a better view of the crowd. He let his gaze roam for half a second—just enough to catch a dark auburn head. Shyanne had come. Just that knowledge sent a buzz of electricity zipping through his bunched muscles. He was seventeen again, participating in his first real match, and Shyanne was in the crowd with a handmade sign, his name written in pink glitter.

Ben—a thickly muscled guy with a man bun—stumbled into position, knocked there by a clothesline.

Dean tensed, prepared for his flying lariat, when his attention caught again on an auburn head—or rather, the sudden disappearance of Shyanne from the crowd.

Dean jumped, his timing off by a few seconds. He didn't quite catch Ben's neck in the crook of his arm and they didn't land gracefully, but thankfully Ben was quick and flexible on the fly. They stumbled together, Ben trying to get Dean in an armlock.

He slipped free and pushed Ben against the ropes, the younger guy attempting to lift him and toss him over the side.

But Dean found himself suddenly distracted. Shyanne hadn't reappeared. There was a small circle of people where he'd seen her last; he saw a blonde that he recognized; one of the cousins, the nice one, but she was kneeling on the ground. Why was she kneeling on the ground?

Then he saw a pair of long legs, prone. What the fuck happened?

Dean abandoned the plan. He slid out of the ring, hearing Ben's confused, "Hey, man," from behind him, since they were supposed to grapple for a few more minutes.

Dean pushed his way into the circle.

Shyanne was on the ground, one leg cocked. Her cousin was fussing over her. Shyanne was pale as fuck but otherwise looked annoyed at the attention.

"I'm fine, Chandler," she said, voice firm and annoyed.

Dean's chest was heaving. "What the fuck happened?"

Shyanne's gaze flicked up and finally met his. There was something there that wasn't reflected in her body language or her words: fear. Why was she afraid?

Chandler was holding her hand and brushing loose hair back off her forehead. Dean knelt down on her other side.

"Just get me up off the floor," Shyanne ground out, offering her free hand to Dean. Chandler's frantic eyes flicked between them both, full of an emotion Dean couldn't name.

Dean nodded towards Shyanne. "I've got her," he said. He slid an arm around her back and lifted her to her feet, Chandler still patting her forehead like she'd fainted. What the fuck?

Dean frowned. "Did you faint?"

Shyanne grimaced, even though she still let Dean take her weight as she got her feet back underneath her. "I didn't faint. I got...a little dizzy and then tripped over these stupid shoes."

She was wearing a pair of brown boots with a tiny heel; not something Dean thought would pose a tripping hazard.

"Do you need to see a doctor?"

"I am a doctor. I'm fine."

Dean grabbed her wrist, checking for a pulse like he knew what the fuck he was doing. There was a slight sheen of sweat on her forehead. Chandler was shorter than Shyanne and stuck herself up under her other arm.

"I'm taking you home."

"I'm fine, I swear."

Dean held on tighter, like Chandler was going to take Shyanne away from him and he was preparing to fight her. "I'll take her home."

Both women looked at him with surprised, wide eyes, like he'd just sprouted a second head. Shyanne's hand tightened in his shirt. "You're in the middle of a match."

Dean shrugged. "I doubt they'll miss me. Some other boys are the main event."

Chandler—who was supposed to be the nice one, the one who liked him—frowned. She looked at Shyanne and the two of them appeared to have some kind of silent conversation that was just communicated through eyebrows.

"Fine," Chandler snapped. "You better text me as soon as you get home. If anything happens to her, Dean Akers, you'll be next."

Dean had to bite the inside of his cheek to keep from smiling at the venom in cute, blonde, bubbly Chandler's voice. She let go of Shyanne with great reluctance.

Despite his big talk, Dean was a professional and avoided burning bridges, if he could help it. He quickly scanned the room over Shyanne's shoulder only to find Teddy already watching them with a slight frown. He tipped his chin up and Teddy did the same.

Dean led them towards the entrance and Shyanne only let them take a few steps before pulling away. She seemed steady on her feet but Dean only let her get so far away; he kept a hold of her hand, which was still slightly clammy in his.

Shyanne inhaled a deep breath. "Do you need to get your stuff?"

"I left most of it in the truck."

Shyanne nodded, her eyes and demeanor feeling a thousand miles away. "You've never left a match before."

Dean opened the passenger side door, gently guiding Shyanne up into the cab, his hands ghosting over her waist and hips, in case she lost her balance again.

She settled into the seat, looking down at him with her dark green eyes, like he was a puzzle she couldn't quite solve.

"No, I've never left a match before," he agreed.

Shyanne was quiet as he drove her home. The orange menace yowled when they came in, rubbing his chunky body around Shyanne's legs. She uncharacteristically ignored him as she walked immediately back to her bedroom.

"Shyanne." He followed her down the hallway. "Shyanne, what the hell was that about?"

She'd pulled off her jacket and tossed it across the bed, another uncharacteristic move. She didn't like things out of their places. Shyanne was standing in front of the window, the streetlights washing out her already pale face.

"Shyanne. Have you been passing out?"

Dean leaned against the doorframe, trying to get his boots unlaced and keep an eye on her at the same time. She'd be pissed as hell if he wore his match boots on her bedroom carpet.

"No," she said, voice quiet.

Dean finally got his boots off. "Then what? I know you said you don't need to go see a doctor, but people just don't faint for no reason."

"I didn't faint," she repeated. "I'm pregnant."

He stumbled, like he'd just taken a punch to the gut, air leaving his lungs in a rush. Shyanne was still facing the window, arms wrapped around herself.

A weird white noise filled Dean's head. He slumped down on the edge of her bed.

Shyanne was still talking, though, like she hadn't just rearranged his entire world with two words.

"We've been shorthanded at the office and I was trying to do interviews and I just ran out of time for lunch. Then I went straight to meet Chandler. I just got a little lightheaded because my blood sugar dropped. I really am fine."

Dean fisted his hands on his knees, barely resisting the urge to hang his head between them. He couldn't catch his breath.

He and Shyanne had never been exclusive. Well, they had never really talked about it. He knew she dated because she'd stop answering his calls sometimes. There was a long stretch in med school with a boyfriend that ultimately didn't last. It was another thing they didn't discuss.

But this changed everything.

"Is that it, then?" he croaked past a dry throat.

Shyanne had been pacing a small circle, but she stopped. "What?"

Dean rubbed his palms up and down his thighs. "Us? Are we done, then?"

Her brow furrowed for a second and then she let out the biggest sigh he'd ever heard. "The baby's yours, you dumbass." She brushed past him, having imploded his whole world again. "I need a drink."

CHAPTER SEVEN
SHYANNE

Standing in front of her tea kettle, Shyanne finally let her hand roam over her belly. The cat was finally out of the bag and she didn't have to pretend there was nothing going on anymore.

Telling Dean didn't exactly go according to plan, but at least that part was over.

His reaction wasn't exactly what she expected, either. It had never crossed her mind that he would assume the baby was someone else's. The simultaneously devastated and terrified look on his face almost had her break out in hysterical laughter, which would have been an inappropriate reaction to the situation, hormones be damned.

She rubbed the side of her stomach. "What are we going to do, hmm, baby?"

"How long?" Dean's strained voice came from behind her.

Shyanne dipped her tea bag into the mug, taking a few seconds to compose herself before turning around.

Dean was in the doorway, arms outstretched, bracing himself on the frame. Like if he didn't, he was liable to topple over.

The sleeves were cut off his shirt, showing off the flex of his biceps, the tendons straining in his forearms. There were dark wings and a delicate angel's face on his bicep; faded red roses down to his wrist.

Damn *fucking* hormones.

Shyanne leaned a hip against the counter. "I'm about three months."

The muscle in his jaw ticked. "You've known for three months and didn't tell me?"

"I haven't seen or talked to you in almost as long, Dean. Were you expecting to be my first call? After everything?"

His expression turned thunderous. "What do you mean, 'everything'? After almost twenty years of loving you, is that everything? After twenty years, you can't even do me the courtesy of one phone call?" His fingers flexed around the wooden frame. "You've gotten everything you've wanted. College, med school, a comfy office, and me to fuck whenever you feel lonely. And I can't even get a phone call from you."

The *you* was almost snarled in his raspy voice, and the vehemence of his words took her aback. But only for a second. Because then fiery hot rage filled all the empty crevices of her soul.

She pushed off the counter. "Fuck you, Dean Akers. You got everything you wanted, too. You *always* put yourself and wrestling first and I never asked you for anything. And that's not going to change now. I don't need anything from you, and neither does this baby."

"That's your fucking problem, Shyanne. You pushed me away when we were eighteen and now you're pushing me away again."

"No! You wanted to go. You never *choose* me."

Dean blinked; color was high in his cheeks. "You never let me choose you." His fingers flexed against the wooden frame before he pushed off. "Always leave before you get left, don't you."

He turned and walked back to her bedroom, leaving Shyanne flustered and confused in his absence.

Before she could carefully organize and categorize her thoughts, Dean walked back in but he had put his boots back on. He didn't look at her as he walked to the door.

He paused with his hand on the knob, knuckles turning white with the force of his grip. "I need some space."

The door snicked shut behind him with little fanfare. Shyanne should have been insulted, or maybe outraged, but all she could feel was a hollow emptiness in her stomach. Because she recognized his parting words. Because she'd said the same thing to him before she moved halfway across the country for residency.

She snatched her mug full of tea off the counter and hurled it to the floor, where it shattered into a mosaic of ceramic shards.

Meatloaf yowled from the living room and glared at her reproachfully.

"Fuck." She grabbed the dish towel off the sink and crouched down, dabbing at the mess.

It was too big. The towel was too small. It was never going to sop up the mess. She couldn't breathe.

Shyanne abandoned the towel in the puddle. She fell back on her ass, pressing up against the counter and pulling her knees to her chest.

She stared into the empty kitchen, seeing nothing. What had Dean meant, she never let him choose her? They both had always had their own hopes and dreams and career aspirations. They orbited each other for as long as possible—Shyanne had even studied kinesiology and sport medicine, had even considered making that her specialty. All in an effort to be closer to him without losing herself.

Shyanne dragged in a heavy breath. Her chest hurt and she didn't want to spend too much time thinking it might be her heart breaking. Because that was illogical and didn't make any sense.

She pulled her phone out of the pocket of her jeans. Chandler had blown up their group chat. Shyanne had forgotten to check in when they'd got home. She sent a quick "I'm fine" text to the group and then pulled up a contact. She only needed one cousin for this.

"I'm not the bad guy here, right?"

"Oh, fuck no."

Micah rubbed Meat's ears aggressively—which he loved—if the biscuits he was making on her thigh were any indication.

Micah had come as soon as Shyanne had called...well, about forty-five minutes later, because that's how long it had taken her to drive all the way to Cedar Creek. Shyanne had spent that time on the floor until her butt was numb. Micah helped her clean up the tea and shards of her mug, wash her face, and put her in a pair of clean pajamas.

Chandler was sweet. She believed in true love and fate and soul mates. She needed someone like Micah, who was as bitter and jaded as she was.

They were in the living room. Micah had made a new cup of tea and Shyanne cradled it between her palms as she sat in the recliner. Micah was with Meat on the couch.

"He said I never let him choose me. That I leave before I get left. That's not true, is it?"

Micah shrugged unhelpfully. "Well, how am I supposed to know? It's not my weird-ass relationship."

Shyanne sipped her tea, staring at the little traitor nestled in Micah's lap. Meat just stared back with content, half-lidded eyes.

Micah coughed, not subtly. "Did you, though, leave him?"

Shyanne wanted to vehemently deny it; she did no such thing. But, if she gave it some thought, there may have been...a few moments.

"Okay, out with it," Micah said. "You look like you've had some kind of personal epiphany."

Shyanne chewed on the inside of her lip. When they were eighteen, she chose to go to a college out-of-state, even though there were plenty of in-state options. It was fine at the time because Dean traveled for wrestling; he'd even been contracted with one of the midsize promotions.

Then there was med school in yet *another* state, and then her residency and the night she told Dean where she'd been accepted.

The midsize promotion had never materialized into the big leagues, and he was back on the indie circuit and between gigs. He had wanted to come with her, had a bag packed and everything, and she had told him she needed space.

"So," Micah drawled. "You *didn't* let him choose you."

Shyanne shook her head. "No, you don't understand. I couldn't let him quit for me. The big leagues could have called him up. There was still a chance at that time. That was our agreement. He was supposed to be making his dreams come true too. I couldn't let him pick me over that."

Micah frowned. "Well, why the hell not? He was a grown man."

Shyanne rubbed her sternum with the heel of her hand. "When my mom was doing my hair for senior prom, she locked eyes with me in the mirror, and told me not to let that boy knock me up and ruin my life."

"Ouch. What a bitch."

"I don't think she really meant it the way I internalized it, you know. Because you know who ruined her life? I did. That was the first and last time we ever talked about it, but I saw her differently after that."

"I'm sorry, Shy. She should have never put that on you."

"It's fine. I was tough enough to handle it then and I'm tough enough to handle it now. I don't have any regrets for the decisions I made, and I didn't want Dean to have any either."

"And that turned out well for you? No regrets? You're so incandescently happy with all your life choices?"

Micah's tone was even, but there was an edge of censure there as well, just a little sharpness that surprised Shyanne.

She took a sip of her now-cold tea, which turned her stomach. She'd never forgotten her mom's face when she'd said those words to her, the sound of her voice. How the moment passed in a brief second filled with so much latent rage and sadness and then her mom had looked away and went back to curling Shyanne's hair.

Shyanne had always been driven to succeed. She always excelled at school, was decent at volleyball, good at most anything she set her mind to. Except, maybe, her romantic relationships.

She couldn't honestly look at the perfect-on-paper life she had built—alone—and say she never regretted any of her choices.

"Micah...I can't. I can't let him choose me now just because of the baby."

Micah sighed loudly and dramatically flopped her head and arms across the back of the couch, scaring Meat off her lap and into the other room. She looked back up. "Babe. When are you going to stop running and finally let that man catch you?"

Chapter Eight

Dean

Dean needed a quiet place to think and that place apparently turned out to be St. Benedict's Catholic Church, just off Main Street in downtown Cedar Creek.

The church was bigger than he remembered growing up.

His grandmother had been aggressively Catholic, his mother less so, but Dean hadn't been involved in organized religion in a very long time.

It probably didn't help that his first gimmick had been The Priest, and he choked guys out with a fake rosary, and then his grandmother disowned him.

He wasn't a religious man, not by any stretch of the imagination, but he was in some sort of existential crisis. He didn't want to go to a bar, where it would be loud and he would be tempted to drown some of his sorrows away. He needed a clear head for this.

He was surprised to find the nave open, but it really wasn't that late at night.

Dean was apparently not the only one in the middle of a crisis, because there was another man a little older than him, kneeling in one of the back pews, his hands clasped in front of him.

He didn't look up as Dean passed him. Dean was headed to the front row, because he felt that would be the most effective strategy. The closer to God and all that.

He sat heavily in the wooden pew, feeling immediately out of place. He was still in his match gear, but he'd managed to pull an old hoodie on at least.

It was pretty, in the church. Candles flickered, casting shadows against the stained glass. It was quiet, too. So quiet he felt like he could hear the pulse of his heartbeat.

He shouldn't have left her house—she'd probably hold that against him too—but he couldn't think straight when she was around. He never could. She was all he thought about; every molecule of his body seemed primed to recognize her presence and drive him mad.

And she was pregnant. And the baby was his. Dean was going to be a father...a title he'd never really put much thought towards.

None of it felt real.

Dean pinched his thigh, just to feel the sting. He was real. His body was real.

And yet.

"You look like you've seen a ghost, my friend," a deep voice rumbled from in front of him.

Dean looked up. And then up some more because the man was massive and built like a brick house. Not really the kind of physique normally seen in clergymen. Dean clocked the man's white collar and black clothes.

He scrubbed his face. "I don't believe in ghosts."

The priest laughed and sat down beside him on the pew. "Neither do I, but you have the look of someone scared shitless. Or someone who's just been given very bad news."

Were priests supposed to cuss? "There's a specific look for that?"

The man nodded solemnly. "Unfortunately, yes. You get used to seeing certain kinds of looks in my line of work."

Dean glanced away. "I suppose that makes sense."

Was he scared shitless? That could be a very succinct and accurate way to describe the feeling currently crawling inside his chest.

He was scared, but not of the baby. He didn't really have much experience with kids, a couple of nieces and nephews he saw occasionally, but that didn't feel like an insurmountable obstacle here.

Shyanne did. The walls she continued to throw up whenever he was around, specifically built just to keep him out. How was he ever supposed to scale them?

They had created a life—together—and still, she was keeping him out, holding him at arm's length.

"So, which one is it?" the priest asked.

Were you supposed to confess to siring a baby out of wedlock to a man of the cloth? Would that go over well?

"A little bit of both, I guess."

The priest nodded sagely. "Why don't we start with something easier first. Your name?"

Dean let out a heavy sigh. "Dean."

"Her name?"

Dean glanced sharply at the priest, who just laughed. He was young, for a priest, Dean thought, and blonde curls flopped over his forehead.

"How did you know?"

"I told you, Dean, there are just certain looks one gets familiar with seeing in my line of work."

Dean rubbed his thighs again. "Shyanne. That's her name." His chest constricted just hearing the syllables leave his mouth. His heart raced, pulse thundered, a thin sheen of sweat broke out on his forehead. Was he having some sort of panic attack?

A large hand thumped him on the back. "Breathe, Dean."

Dean sucked in air, his lungs burning with the effort. "I don't know what I'm supposed to do, man. There's almost a whole lifetime of hurt between us. Of mistakes. I don't know how I'm supposed to fix that."

"Maybe you should stop trying to fix it."

Dean barked out a short laugh. "I don't think that will go over well, Father."

"Has it worked? Fixing it?" There was a soft smile on the priest's face, like he knew something Dean didn't, but that was probably true. There were many things Dean didn't know.

"No," he admitted.

"Then maybe it's time to try something else. You love her, right?" Dean nodded. That much, he could admit to the other man. "You know what they say about love? 'Love bears all things, believes all things, hopes all things, endures all things.'"

Dean frowned. "Is that a Bible quote?" It sure sounded like one and Dean could almost swear he'd seen the same sentiment embroidered on a pillow somewhere.

"It's kind of part of the job description," the priest said. "Dispensing wisdom via scripture."

"Do they quiz you in priest school?"

"They sure do."

Dean found himself smiling, just a bit, despite the tightness in his chest.

So, love endured all things. But Dean didn't know if he could. However, he wasn't about to give up until he tried.

He had spent years losing Shyanne over and over and over again. And he was done enduring that.

Later, Dean would have to have a talk with her about leaving her front door unlocked. But, for now, he was grateful he could just barge back into her house.

Shyanne was in the living room, curled up in the big leather armchair, wrapped in a fuzzy blanket. Her eyes were red-rimmed and her cheeks were puffy. Micah, the cousin who hated him, was on the couch with the cat.

Shyanne stopped mid-sniffle, face going slack with surprise. "Dean, what—"

"No," he cut her off. "I'm done, Shyanne. I'm done pretending I don't want you, that I don't love you. I've loved you since we were fourteen and you gave Malcolm Fenny a black eye because he grabbed your ass in Geometry."

He heard Micah snort-laugh. "Classic."

The color drained from Shyanne's face. Well, his proclamation had been a tad bit more aggressive than he'd rehearsed on the drive back over. The speech he rehearsed was measured, reasonable, full of platitudes and pauses for Shyanne to interject and express her own feelings. But he was so tired of not being able to say it.

"Well," Micah said, lifting the orange cat off her lap and placing him on the floor, where he huffed. "I think that's my cue to go."

Shyanne's panicked eyes flicked to her cousin, as if she was pleading with her not to go.

Micah left anyway.

She patted Dean's shoulder on her way through the arch. "I was always Team Dean, you know."

Dean felt his lips quirk in a grin, but quickly sobered his expression when Shyanne frowned at her cousin's back.

He heard the front door shut and let out a quick breath. He moved to take a step forward, but the damn cat curled around his ankles and he stumbled.

"Fucking cat."

Shyanne's jaw flexed, like she'd bitten the inside of her cheek. Maybe all hope wasn't lost. Dean leaned down and scooped the cat up, flipping him over and sticking him in the crook of his arm, like a baby. The cat purred contentedly, eyes closed.

"He never lets me do that," she said, voice hoarse.

"He just likes me better, I guess." Dean rubbed the cat's fat belly aggressively, which only made the menace purr louder.

Shyanne sighed, pulling the blanket tighter around her shoulders. Her coppery hair was a mess, like the blanket had been over her head at one point.

"Why did you come back?" Her eyes darted away, landing on anything and everything except for his face.

"I always come back, Tater."

She let out a small, strangled, broken sob, burying her face in her hands.

Oh, fuck, he was making her cry again. Dean dropped the cat, who landed on his feet with an affronted yowl before scurrying away.

In two steps, he was on his knees in front of her, tugging on her wrists so he could see her face. Her eyes were glazed and red-rimmed, but no tears made their way down her cheeks.

"I'm sorry," she said.

"For what?"

Her bottom lip trembled. "I should have told you sooner."

Dean's hands tightened on her wrists; the bones felt so delicate under his palms. She was always so hard, so tough, on the outside.

Even now, he could tell she was reining in her emotions, respooling the unraveling threads. She pulled in steadying, regular breaths through her nose, blinking slowly, clearing her eyes. Her arms stopped quivering as he watched.

"I need to show you something," Dean said, releasing her hands and standing back up. He started unbuttoning his pants and Shyanne choked on something that would have been a shocked laugh in any other situation.

Instead, she just narrowed her eyes. "I've seen your dick, Dean."

"I'm not showing you my dick," he mumbled, pulling his pants and briefs down just enough to expose an expanse of skin on his pelvis.

Shyanne's gaze darted around—almost panicked—before she finally looked at the spot he indicated.

Her brow creased in confusion. "What am I looking at?"

Dean ran two fingers over the tattoo. "It's a potato."

Shyanne's jaw went slack. "What? No, it isn't."

"Yes, it is. Although, it looked better years ago." Now, it just kind of looked like a grayish spot on his skin. Not his best tattoo or his worst, unfortunately.

She blinked owlishly at the tattoo and then back up at his face. Dean pulled up his pants, as if that settled the whole matter, and for him, it did.

"You're it for me, Shyanne. You always have been. I meant what I said, earlier. I love you. I should have told you a hundred times over—" Dean abruptly shut his mouth because Shyanne had turned an alarming shade of ghostly white.

She put a hand over her mouth. "I think I'm going to be sick."

CHAPTER NINE
SHYANNE

Shyanne dry-heaved into the toilet, suddenly very thankful that she kept to a regular cleaning schedule and didn't skip any days.

She had been lucky with her pregnancy symptoms so far—horny and emotional at the wrong times, mild nausea that came and went, usually without any incident.

Her stomach spasmed again but nothing came up, which was almost worse than actually vomiting.

She heard the bathroom sink start running and closed her eyes, pressing her forehead into the seat.

She physically felt Dean kneel down beside her; his presence was sucking all the air from the room, from her lungs, the heat from his body searing into hers.

He brushed loose hair off the back of her neck and then replaced his warm fingers with a cool washcloth.

"I thought morning sickness was supposed to happen in the morning."

"A common misconception."

"Noted."

"Why are you still here? I'm gross."

His large, firm hand rubbed circles in her back and Shyanne had to resist the urge to just melt into a puddle on the bathroom floor.

"Remember in eleventh grade when we swapped strep throat back and forth for almost five months because we wouldn't stop making out? That was worse than this."

Shyanne snorted and then had to hang her head deeper into the bowl as her throat spasmed. Dean's voice was warm and fond and his touch so secure, so safe. She wanted to cry but also hit something in frustration.

"I ruined your speech."

He huffed a laugh. "I can start over, if you want."

Shyanne took several deep breaths through her nose. A headache had started to accompany the nausea, probably from ineffectually heaving into the toilet.

"I feel gross. Will you just...help me get in the shower?" She felt guilty and extremely selfish for even asking Dean to stay and help her, but between the lightheadedness earlier and now the nausea, it felt almost riskier for her to be alone.

Dean bundled her up and helped her stand for the second time tonight. "Are you sure you don't need to go see someone?"

Shyanne shook her head, hanging on to his taut biceps for what felt like dear life. "I'll call my OB in the morning. I just want to get clean."

His hands slid up her arms, her neck, until he cupped both cheeks in his palms. His brown eyes searched hers, for just a moment, before he tipped her head down and kissed her forehead.

Then, he set to work.

He started the shower, checking the temp, even as water splashed on his clothes.

He undressed her, hands landing on odd places on her body, like he was checking her over for wounds, fingers lingering for a millisecond on her stomach.

Then, he turned to go.

"Wait." Shyanne's voice was hoarse; she cleared her throat and tried again. "Wait, Dean. I know we still have a lot to talk about but will you...shower with me? Just...because?" She wasn't feeling particularly amorous right now, but she also didn't want to be alone. Which a new, unexpected feeling for her. She was strong enough; being alone never used to bother her.

Dean's brow furrowed, and she knew she was allover the place with her words, her emotions, her demands of him.

But then he nodded, once, and started removing his own clothes.

Shyanne's gaze strayed to the tattoo he'd revealed to her earlier, and her chest tightened. It only looked like a potato if she squinted her eyes. She wondered when he got it, because it definitely wasn't fresh. Dean was heavily tattooed, the majority of them black and gray, so the little potato must have just blended into the others. She had stopped noticing new tattoos years ago, especially the smaller ones.

Dean held open the glass door for her, his other hand brushing across her elbow as they stepped into the spray together.

Her remodeled shower was bigger than it would have been before, but it was still a tight fit for the both of them.

There wasn't enough room for them not to touch, wet skin sliding over wet skin. Shyanne was in front. At first, she was facing away from him, but Dean quickly turned her around and made her tip her head back into the water, a hand combing through her loose hair. The hot water felt like heaven on her sweaty skin.

She closed her eyes and let Dean tend to her. He washed her hair, grumbling about how long it took to get all the suds out. His hands slid across her body as he reached for the loofah and her body wash, causing her breath to hitch slightly.

The scratch of the loofah tingled around her shoulders, her collarbones, down her spine, over the curve of her ass.

She tightened her arms around Dean's corded neck, pulling their bodies closer before she opened her eyes.

His brown eyes were blown almost black with desire, his sultry lips parted, his tender ministrations paused on her hip. She caught a look of unbridled wanting before he quickly shuttered his expression, frowning at her severely, those plush lips hardening, even as his body told a different story.

"No," he scolded. "Not until you've eaten something."

She slid her palms across his shoulders. "I did eat something, while you were gone." She didn't mean anything by it, but Dean flinched anyway at the reminder of his brief absence earlier.

Shyanne traced the hard lines of his throat, the sculpted edges of his jaw, the fine line of his nose. He sighed into her touch, his body molding to the front of hers, the loofah dropped and forgotten as he clutched at her hips, pressing her center to his.

Dean let out a strangled groan, burying his nose in her wet hair. Shyanne inhaled his scent, tempting and tangled in hers, her lips brushing against his throat.

"I want you," she said. It was less than he deserved, but all that she could manage. He had bared his soul to her, so why was it so hard for her to reciprocate? It felt like there was a weight in her chest, in her throat, that kept her real feelings from spewing out.

She defaulted to what was safe: sex. Even as Dean demanded more from her.

"Hold on," he rasped, hiking up one of her legs and bracing her foot on one of the inlaid shower ledges.

Shyanne's breathing quickened, her body trembling in anticipation. His wet palm slid up her thigh and then slipped between their bodies. He didn't waste time with teasing strokes, his sure fingers finding and circling her clit.

She shuddered, pressing tighter against him. His other hand was firm on the small of her back, to keep them both steady. Shyanne captured his mouth with hers, softly kissing him as he fingered her. Dean sighed into her mouth, and for a few moments, they breathed each other's air.

The orgasm built quickly because Dean knew her body, knew exactly how much pressure to apply, when to change the pace and when to push her to her limits.

He slid two fingers inside her and Shyanne came all over his hand, her fingers digging into the back of his neck.

Dean hummed deep in the back of his throat, sucking at her jaw. "Now, we have to get clean again. Where's the loofah?" He patted her hips like they were pants with pockets that would magically hold the elusive loofah.

"You dropped it." Shyanne went to bend over and retrieve the loofah from the floor of the shower, but Dean stopped her with a hand on her arm.

"I'm not responsible for what happens if you bend over in front of me."

She choked on a short laugh. "You get it, then."

They switched places, in a concentrated dance of wet and slippery limbs. Dean bent to grab the loofah, the tight muscles in his thighs and ass bunching. She couldn't resist. Shyanne ran a hand over his sculpted flank. If she was grateful for wrestling for only one thing, it would be Dean's round ass.

He smirked at her over his shoulder as he straightened.

They had been in the shower so long the water was starting to cool. Dean made quick work washing his own body and what little hair he had on his head. Shyanne shivered, goose bumps running up her arms, when he turned off the knob.

They got out, Dean wrapping a towel around his hips, one around her shoulders, and one on her hair, which Shyanne had to redo.

He grabbed a bottle of her favorite lotion off the counter and herded her back into the bedroom. His palm was hot on her back; Shyanne adjusted the towel around her breasts.

"Lie down."

She huffed, but did as he said anyway, laying down on her back on top of the duvet.

Dean sat at her feet, pulling both her legs onto his lap.

"I'm okay now," she said, staring at the ceiling, trying, valiantly, to ignore the heat still coiled in her belly. There was no trace of nausea anymore, not when her body and her blood were buzzing with him.

"What's your point?"

She heard the squirt of the lotion, a brief pause, and then Dean's hot, firm, slick hands closed over one of her feet, thumbs digging into the arch.

Shyanne moaned, her whole body shuddering.

He laughed. "I don't think I've ever heard that sound before. Even during sex."

Her eyes fluttered closed, arms falling limp at her sides. "This is better than sex."

He chuckled again and they lapsed into a comfortable silence as his hands did magical things to her feet. Then her ankles and calves. It felt like he was massaging years' worth of tension out of her body.

Shyanne moved her hands to her stomach, picking at the soft material of the towel. "You don't have to be involved, you know, if you don't want to. I wanted you to know, of course, but I don't expect anything from you." She was surprised that all the words came out clearly. Maybe it was because she said them at the ceiling and not to his face.

The movement of his hands stilled. "Why would you say that to me?"

A spark of anger lanced through her chest, ruining all the warm, fuzzy feelings from her orgasm and foot massage.

"Because, Dean. It's not like we planned this. It's not like we're together. You travel all the time, all over the country, and sometimes *out* of the country. We never even talked about...about kids, ever. I want this baby, with or without you, and I would never force you into anything you didn't want." There. She'd told her bedroom ceiling all the dark, confusing things that were in her heart.

He sighed. "Did you even listen to anything I said in the past hour? God, you're so fucking hardheaded."

Shyanne pushed up on her elbows, indignant.

Dean was scrubbing beleaguered hands over his face. He was perched on the edge of the bed, one leg pulled up, the towel rouching up his thighs.

He pulled his hands down and stared at her with hard eyes, his expression a potent combination of anger, frustration, and a deep longing.

"I love you, Shyanne fucking Bennett. And you're out of your goddamn mind if you think I don't want this baby. Because they're a part of you, a part of us. And guess fucking what? You're mine. And so are they."

The last part of his declaration was practically growled at her, his dark eyes flashing, a ruddiness rising to his cheeks. He grabbed the end of her towel, and she knew it was a threat, a promise...and both of those things sent fire cracking up her spine.

She licked her lips, suddenly finding it very hard to breathe, to think, to find any counters to his arguments.

He tugged on the towel. "Tell me now. Tell me that you don't love me. That you don't want me. Do it."

She didn't.

Because she couldn't.

And he knew it.

CHAPTER TEN
DEAN

Shyanne stared at him with wide eyes, a dark flush on her cheeks that dripped down her throat and crawled along her collarbones.

Her chest rose and fell with short, sharp breaths.

He crushed the edge of her light purple towel in his fist, inching it down further until the tops of her breasts were exposed.

Did she really think he wouldn't want anything to do with their child? After all this time, that's what she thought of him? Or was it just another way to keep him at a distance?

If that were true, then he had several things to prove to her. And he would start tonight and continue until there were no doubts left in her mind, about anything.

"Nothing to say?" He practically growled at her, feeling heat rise to his own face, flood his stomach, tighten his balls.

She remained silent, the tip of her wet tongue pushing at her bottom lip.

Dean hummed as the towel slipped lower and lower, exposing each rosy nipple. They were already taut, tits heaving with her labored breathing. He hadn't been wrong. Each sweet globe was bigger. A strange feeling constricted his chest; Shyanne was very early in her pregnancy. Her body would only grow plumper and rounder as she grew their child. Months and months of heavy breasts and a round belly. The thought stole his breath.

He'd never had a kink for pregnant women before, but apparently when it came to Shyanne, there was nothing she could be or not be, do or not do, that made him want her any less.

The towel rasped across her belly, down her hips and thighs, until she was completely bare before him. Her mound was covered in copper ringlets, several shades darker than her hair. Her thighs parted under his perusal, pink lips already damp. Her limbs trembled.

"Look at you. You think you don't belong to me? That your body doesn't belong to me? I haven't even touched you yet and you're drenched. Your pretty cunt knows who owns it." Dean's cock was hard and leaking against his thigh. He had her body, he always knew that, but he wanted it all. Her heart, her mind, her temper, the sardonic tilt of her mouth when she secretly thought he was funny but didn't want to admit it.

Shyanne fell back against the pillows with a groaned, "Oh, God." The towel around her hair had come undone, the wild strands spilling free.

Dean stood, letting his own towel fall off his hips, before resettling on the bed between her legs. He grabbed Shyanne's hips and pulled her down, draping her thighs over his. He could feel the heat from her pussy on his cock and his whole body ached.

He grabbed the lotion again, coating his hands, and rubbed them over her thighs, the soft spots between her thighs and stomach, and over her belly.

She gazed at him—suspiciously quiet—with hooded eyes, her whole body flushing red. The freckles across her chest and down her sternum almost disappeared under the blush.

"You know," he said, gliding his hands up to her breasts. "I can't wait until you start showing. Then, everyone will know who fucks you. Who came inside you."

She made a frantic little mewling sound in the back of her throat, back arching, dripping onto the bed.

He pinched her nipples, rolling the taut buds between his fingertips. "Liked that, did you?" With a short thrust of his hips, he ran the length of his shaft through her folds.

"Want me to do it again?" He pressed his forehead to hers. "Fill you up until your sweet pussy can't hold any more?"

She huffed and bit his ear. "Do it then and stop talking. Or do you just like to hear the sound of your own voice?" Her words were caustic but her voice was low and raspy.

He grinned down at her, sliding one hand backdown between their bodies until he felt her slick skin.

Shyanne gasped as he slid a finger inside. She was hot and frenzied and squirming underneath him. Her nails dug into his biceps. A line appeared between her brows as she writhed on his hand. He kissed it away.

"Dean, Dean," she moaned, his name falling out of her mouth like a plea. "Dean, what are you doing?"

He kissed a line down her jaw. "Fucking you, baby."

She practically growled at him, her thighs squeezing his hips. He circled her clit with his finger.

"No, you're, fuck, you're just—" she cut off with a moan and a full body shiver as the small orgasm rolled through her. Her limbs relaxed marginally, but he wasn't done with her yet.

Dean captured her swollen mouth with his, and kissed her like he had all the time in the world. Because now he did. Because he wasn't letting her go anymore.

He kissed her until her arousal dried on his fingers.

He kissed her until she let out a very unlike-Shyanne dreamy sigh, her hands tangling together behind his head.

Dean rubbed his nose against her, against the bone of her cheek. Shyanne nuzzled into his neck, her lips brushing against his pulse.

Dean adjusted his hips, lining his aching cock up with Shyanne's hot entrance. With a gentle thrust, he sank inside a few careful inches. Her breathing hitched and he felt her teeth on his neck. He buried one of his fists in her hair, tilting her head back.

She gasped, her heels digging into the back of his calves. It was a wordless plea for him to go faster, but Dean wanted to take his time, savor her, watch every expression flit over her face.

The way her eyes widened and her pupils dilated as he slid further inside, his hardness splitting her soft flesh. Her teeth digging into her plump lower lip. The flare of her nostrils with frustration. She tried to buck her hips, but the position they were in, him so completely laying over her body, didn't allow for much movement.

For years, they had just been fucking, fast and hard and furious and he wanted to start something different, to create something new between them. If she didn't believe the words he said, maybe she'd believe him if he didn't use his words.

She freed her lip and her mouth opened on a moan as he bottomed out inside her. Her cunt spasmed around him, hot and hungry and greedy, as she writhed under him, nails digging into his shoulder blades.

Dean started an inexorably slow gyration, honestly, he was barely moving, but his breath came ragged and short like he was running.

It was pure torture to move so slowly, but he wanted to savor each stroke, each exhalation of angry breath from Shyanne, each hitch as he put pressure on her hair.

He loved the feel of his bare skin against the inside of her body. He could feel every flutter. He'd always loved feeling her come, feeling the reaction of her body when he came inside her. He'd be able to come inside her over and over and over again for months with no consequences. The very thought of filling her up over and over again, of watching his cum drip down her thighs, sent a spark up his spine.

Dean groaned, thighs and back muscles aching.

"Dean," she gasped. "Dean, what are you doing?" she asked him again. But this time her voice was filled with something urgent, vulnerable.

A ragged moan dragged out of his throat. He wasn't going to last much longer like this.

Making love to you, he thought, but didn't say. Even in his head, the statement sounded too trite, a cliché he'd never believed in, like the plot of some romantic comedy.

Regular people didn't make love, did they? But he didn't have any other words for what they were doing, what they had done. Shyanne was pregnant; they had made a *baby*, for fuck's sake.

Dean dragged in a labored breath; his chest felt tight. He made a strange noise; his throat cramped. Something was happening to his body.

Shyanne grabbed his face in both of her hands and made him make eye contact with her. There was a strange expression on her face; something odd between pleasure and concern.

Because he was still fucking her. He may behaving some kind of heart attack or panic attack or something, but he wasn't going to stop.

With a hard push of his arms, he sat back on his heels, pulling Shyanne with him, his cock still inside her.

They both grunted at the change in position. She was above him, seated on his lap, her legs automatically wrapping around his hips.

"Oh my God," she whispered, burying her head in his neck.

He did the same, hands running up and down her spine, inhaling her, the fresh, clean, soft scent of her soap.

A few upward thrusts and he was done.

His orgasm ripped through his lower body, making every limb shiver with the release. Shyanne came seconds later, her cunt clamping down on his cock as her teeth sunk into his trapezius.

Dean's chest heaved; he still felt like he couldn't fill his lungs. Shyanne's shoulder was wet. He felt his cum leaking from her and onto his pelvis and thighs.

She was running her hands over his neck and head. He finally tipped his head back so he could look up at her. He had to blink away the tears that had glued his lashes together.

Shyanne looked about as startled as he felt. Crying during sex was a new one, but at least he wasn't dying.

Dean finally inhaled a deep breath, focusing his attention on her deep green eyes. Those eyes were everything, she was everything.

"Are you okay?" She cupped his face, thumbs brushing at the tears on his cheeks.

His eyes were hot, but his heart felt lighter. Shyanne peppered his wet face with kisses. "I can't," she whispered against his jaw.

Dean's throat tightened. "Can't what?"

She sighed. "Can't tell you I don't love you."

Dean brushed one hand through her damp hair, while the other trailed down her back, settling just above her hips, to keep her pressed to him. "Then don't, baby. Let me love you. Let me choose you." His palm slid over her hip to settle on her stomach. "Let me choose them."

Shyanne's adorable freckled nose wrinkled. "What about your career?"

Dean barked out a laugh. "I think I'm getting a little old to voluntarily be pummeled with light tubes, don't you agree?" His thumb rubbed circles over her skin.

She chewed her lip. "What if you hate me...after?"

"I won't."

"How can you be so sure?"

Dean gripped her hip and thrust upward; Shyanne gasped as she bounced. He was still inside her, cum pooling between their joined bodies, and she'd been dithering so long he was growing hard again.

"I've only been sure about one thing in my life, Shyanne. You. I should have picked you when we were eighteen, but I didn't because I was young and a dumbass. I love you. I love you, Tater."

Shyanne's lips had parted and the lower one trembled slightly; bright red color stained her cheek bones. "Dean, I won't survive losing you again. I won't and I can't. I refuse." Her voice quaked, but her words were laced with her signature steel.

He chuckled and ghosted a kiss over her lips. "I can't promise you perfect. I can't promise that you won't get pissed at me or I won't get fed up with your attitude." She frowned and he kissed the line between her brows. "But I can promise that I will spend every day loving you and choosing the life that we build. Together." He emphasized the last word with an undulation of his hips and Shyanne inhaled sharply.

She twined her arms around his neck. The tips of their noses touched and Dean's vision blurred as he tried to maintain eye contact.

Her lips brushed his and a thousand tiny pinpricks of heat zipped through his body. "I love you," she said, the words soft and sultry and so heavy, they felt weighted against his mouth.

"I love you," he told her again, and he wanted to laugh with exhilaration, with joy, with pleasure. Because he'd get to love her for the rest of their lives.

Epilogue

The piercing cry of their four-month-old woke Shyanne with a start.

She always woke up startled when Opal Bennett-Akers cried, as if her body and mind hadn't quite gotten used to the angry, demanding little life she'd brought into this world.

Shyanne rolled over with a groan, to already find the other side of the bed empty. Not a minute later, Dean walked into the bedroom, a pair of athletic shorts slung low on his hips, a warm bottle already in hand.

"Why so upset, my little unemployed freeloader," he cooed over the bassinet.

The wailing stopped as soon as he leaned over, replaced immediately by a bubbling gurgle.

"Shit your pants, huh? Well, I'd be pissed off too." Dean set the bottle on the dresser, scooped Opal up, and left the room, presumably to go to the changing table, which was in *her* room. Which was where she was supposed to be too.

But they'd moved the bassinet into their bedroom because Opal apparently hated sleep, hated swaddling, hated her crib, and hated Shyanne...or just enjoyed terrorizing Shyanne with bouts of two-hour wailing sessions, she couldn't decide.

Dean, on the other hand, had stepped into the role of father like it was as easy as putting on a new coat. Micah and Chandler had brought him a mug that said "World's Greatest Dad" to the hospital, and he apparently took that title very seriously.

He handled most of the overnight feedings, and he napped with Opal on his chest during the day while Shyanne answered emails from the office. Their lips pursed in exactly the same way while asleep and her phone was filled with a montage of sleeping pics.

He'd brought her snacks and made lactation cookies when she was breastfeeding. When she finally said *fuck breastfeeding*, after three torturous weeks of low supply, hours of fruitless pumping, simultaneous crying sessions (both her and Opal), he'd run out and bought bottles, sanitizing equipment, and a formula mixer. He had developed a strict bottle and nipple rotation and frowned at Shyanne whenever she messed it up.

When her postpartum anxiety got bad, he made her leave the house and go to the library or the bookstore or the coffee shop. Shyanne might have created life, sustained life, birthed life, but Dean was the miracle.

She felt the bed dip, and a sleeping, sated Opal was placed in the middle. Dean had cleared a spot for her, moving away the blankets and pillows.

Opal sprawled like a starfish, smelling like baby powder. Shyanne inched her face closer, sticking her nose on Opal's downy forehead and inhaling.

Dean laid down on the baby's other side, his hand ghosting over her plump middle.

"She's not supposed to be in the bed," Shyanne said.

"That's what you said about the bassinet."

Shyanne just hummed, caressing Opal's palm until the baby's fingers latched onto hers. Her chest constricted.

"How do you do it?"

"Do what?" Dean's voice was a sleepy rasp. He was tired, but he never complained.

"Be God's gift to parenting." Shyanne's voice came out petulant, but she'd blame that on being severely sleep deprived.

Dean chuckled, his hand resting lightly on Opal's chest, rising with her slow breaths. Shyanne knew what he was doing because she did it too—checking to make sure the baby was still alive.

"I'm not. I'm scared shitless most days."

"I'm the world's worst mom."

Dean popped up from the other side, practically glaring at her over Opal's peacefully sleeping, footie-pajama-wrapped body.

"Don't say that shit. I watched them cut you open, sew you back up, and then send you home with a nine-pound baby. You're the strongest thing on Earth."

Shyanne had to close her eyes as the pressure of tears threatened to overwhelm her. "I'm ready to go back to work," she whispered, like it was a confession or some kind of dark, deep secret that shouldn't be revealed.

"And?"

"I *want* to go back to work." She missed her routines, her work, her patients. She loved her job. She had fought and clawed for her job. She was looking forward to the end of her maternity leave; she was ready to reclaim that part of herself, of her identity. And the guilt was an intense, ugly, toxic creature that had taken root in her chest.

She felt Dean's warm palm on her forehead, brushing back through her hair. The tears slipped out of the corners of her eyes.

"You are the perfect mom for her. This world is a complete trash fire. She needs a mom like you. Strong. Fierce. Uncompromising. Stubborn as a fucking rock."

Shyanne choked on a laugh, even as tears rolled down her cheeks.

"You just go out and make that money, baby, and we'll be here when you get home." True to his word, Dean had given up wrestling and his big-league dreams for her. For their daughter, their little family.

Shyanne snorted again, feeling some of the ever-present knot in her chest ease. Opal's nose scrunched up like she was getting ready to cry again. Shyanne shushed Dean, and ran her hand over the baby's forehead, her small nose, her devastatingly soft cheeks until she settled again.

Dean had flopped back down on his side. "I wasn't even talking that loud," he stage-whispered.

There was a chastising *brrp* as Meatloaf joined them on the bed, flicking the end of his tail. He walked over Dean's stomach—who grunted—and flopped at Opal's feet and started a gentle biscuit-making session on her soles.

Opal didn't stir. Meat gave her an experimental sniff and then rolled over, belly up, his desires clear.

If only she could read her baby as well as she could read her cat.

Shyanne aggressively rubbed the cat's chunky belly as he purred. She felt almost at peace, settled more in her own skin, as pre-dawn light crept through a crack in the window. She knew she'd be okay, be whole again, if not in this exact moment, or tomorrow, or the next day, but eventually, one day. Because she had her perfect little family.

She felt Dean's hand on her head. "Sleep when the baby sleeps, Tater. I've got you."

And she knew he did.

Her body and her heart were safe with him.

So, she closed her eyes and slept.

Afterword

Thank you for reading *Main Event*!

I hope you enjoyed Shyanne, Dean, and Opal's story and are ready to prop up your feet and stay for a long time in Cedar Creek, Kentucky. A good time is guaranteed!

Reviews are one of the best ways to support an author, so I would love you forever if you left one (or even just some stars!) somewhere on the internet (also, tell you friends about the BPC!).

Be sure you're following me for updates about the series. Who's next? You'll just have to wait and see!

Did you really, *really* enjoy this story and want to dive deeper into the Jessica-verse?

I would be absolutely tickled if you joined me on Patreon! You can get free eBooks, sticker mailings, be-hind-the-scenes updates, bonus content, early access, and can start reading my unhinged paranormal romance serial, *Guilty As Sin*.

About the Author

J.L. Minyard is the not-so-secret pen name of award-winning young adult author Jessica Minyard. Jessica is an author, poet, ISTJ, Sagittarius, and boy mom who lives and writes from the bluegrass.

Check out both her contemporary series:

Penn Warren University

Bluegrass Performance Center

For freebies, sneak peeks, and other updates, head to jessicaminyard.com to sign up for her newsletter or join her Facebook group or Patreon.

Follow her on social media:

facebook.com/jessicaminyardbooks

instagram.com/callmeshashka

tiktok.com/@jessicawritesromance

amazon.com/stores/J.L.-Minyard/author/B0B7R171CP

Minyard's Minions